Burn Out
An Animal Communicator Mystery

Also by Victoria Heckman

K.O.' in Honolulu
K.O.'d in the Volcano
K.O.'d in the Rift
K.O.'d in the Big Surf (2011)

Kapu-Sacred

Burn Out
An Animal Communicator Mystery

Victoria Heckman

This is a work of fiction, a product of the author's imagination. Any resemblance to specific locales, events, or persons living or dead is entirely coincidental.

2010 Revenge Publishing
Copyright 2010 Victoria Heckman
All rights reserved.
Published in the United States by Revenge Publishing.
ISBN 978-0-9846098-1-9
Cover Design: Liam Heckman
Author photo: Blue Moon Photography

For Fire Fighters Everywhere

Acknowledgements

Gratitude goes to my expert readers without whom this book would not be as accurate. All errors are my own. Thank you to Captain Dave Doust (Ret.) in the Toronto, Canada Fire Department and to Captain Howard Sanford of the Cayucos Fire Protection District. They both read meticulously and corrected my terms and procedures. I had to modify some things for the plot, but they tried to keep me straight. Also, thank you to emergency room physician Eric Jacobsen for checking my medical sections.

My Sisters in Crime--Central Coast Chapter buddies are always incredible and supportive. Also, my extra special editor, Margaret Searles; I couldn't do it without you.

Finally, thank you to my family for their patience and support with all the lonely, and often painful, aspects of living with a writer.

Author's Note:

I have set this book in mythical towns but I'd like to say that in all of my dealings with numerous fire departments and all their personnel, I was always met with professionalism and courtesy. So no, none of the "bad" people are you.

One

She's dead.

Elizabeth Murphy sat in her favorite white wicker chair, sipping her first cup of Peet's coffee.

She's dead.

I know, Elizabeth replied in her head. *I'm sorry.*

Elizabeth looked out the picture window. Its view was the lovely garden her husband Tig had created for her between his shifts as a fire fighter. Today, a dead mourning dove lay on the walk. Another dove sat on the telephone wire that ran from the pole at the corner of the yard, over the walk, to the house.

I'll take care of her, Elizabeth thought.

And? said the other dove.

I'll make the window more visible to you. I am really sorry.

For what? The dove flew away.

"Some birds!" Elizabeth closed her eyes, brown curly hair dropping around her pale face, and began her morning meditation.

After rousing herself from her relaxed state, she pulled on a pair of latex gloves, one of many she kept stashed in her house and car. Out the back door, she walked to where the dove lay.

What are you doing?

"Shh, not now," said Elizabeth.

I was going to eat that.

"No, you're not." Elizabeth knelt, cradled the small gray bird and regarded the speaker, her large neutered male tabby cat, Teddy. "I know that's nature and all, but it's gross. Besides, I got it first."

Fair enough.

Teddy followed Elizabeth out the back gate to a rough undeveloped area of land she and Tig affectionately called "the outback."

Although this little California beach town was about as far from Australia as it could be, "the outback" was wild enough for Elizabeth. Deer trails criss-crossed the hillside acres and wildlife pulsed just beyond the row of subdivision homes. She and Tig often walked these trails and had spied deer, bob cats, coyotes, hares, rabbits, snakes, lizards, many birds and insects plus myriad plants she could not name. Her area was animals and Tig's was plants. She often teased him, calling him the 'plant whisperer' because he could touch or sometimes merely look at a plant and know it had life in it. She joked she was the 'plant murderer' and therefore they were the perfect team.

Elizabeth dug a hole with her hand and gently laid the bird inside. Teddy watched, unblinking.

"I don't think so." Elizabeth re-filled the hole, picked up a large rock and set it atop the fresh dirt. "Good luck digging that out."

Teddy eyed her narrowly. With a flip of his tail, he turned and sauntered back through the open gate.

She followed him to the house and heard the front door open as she reached the kitchen.

"I'm home," called her husband.

Elizabeth greeted him with a kiss. He still smelled of smoke, although he always showered at the station after a fire. She liked the smell. It was so *him*.

"Long night?" She followed him back to their bedroom. He would take another shower and change clothes again, trying to separate himself from work.

"Warehouse fire. Total loss. The captain wanted us to go in. Whole thing's in flames, no one to save, the roof's gonna cave, but he wants us in."

Elizabeth smiled, knowing what was coming. Her husband was something of a rascal; one of the reasons she loved him.

"I told him sure, the roof's going to collapse any second. Right after you. He was about to give me shit for insubordination, but then the roof fell in. He didn't have anything to say after that." Tig finished his story from the bathroom and the shower started.

"Breakfast?" she poked her head in. Her heart beat a little faster to see him there, tall, with dark, curly hair, impatiently waiting for the water to heat.

"Yeah, I'm starved."

"Me, too." He caught her lascivious wink and laughed while he stepped into the shower.

"Later, you!" he called over the spray.

Elizabeth returned to the kitchen and made

11

apple waffles and sausage. She was pouring his coffee when he appeared in his favorite surfing tee shirt and old jeans.

"Let's eat by the pond. Grab the syrup," she said, balancing two plates and his coffee cup.

They sat at the patio table near the koi pond and ate silently. Elizabeth knew Tig was starved after a long shift, no matter how much he seemed to eat. This had been his 24 hour shift, when she missed him the most, but that also meant he'd be home for several days now.

He had eaten four pancakes to her one when he came up for air. "I was so hungry. This is great."

"You always say that!"

"It's always true. What's your day like today?"

"I have two horses to see in the north county."

"What's the problem?" Tig finished his last bites of sausage and pancake.

"Not sure. Two older 'retired' horses, rescues, but they've been together a year and now aren't getting along."

"How come you're not doing it over the phone?"

Elizabeth had so many calls for advice on animal behavior that she sometimes did respond by phone. She preferred to see the animals in person, but distance or scheduling didn't always make that possible.

"I don't get many calls for horses so I want to see them. You know how I feel about horses."

12

He did. "Last time you didn't wash that sweater for a week because you like the horsey smell."

Elizabeth got up to clear the dishes. "A girl's gotta sleep with something when her husband is out all night."

He slapped her gently on the rear and rose to help her.

Two

Elizabeth wound her way through oak studded hills and several ranches before she found the place she sought. She nosed her little car down an extremely steep and oddly canted drive into a neat gated yard with a barn and paddock. Her clients waited in the paddock: a huge bay stallion and a smaller chestnut mare. Their person waited by the gate.

Elizabeth rolled down her window. "Is it okay if I park here?"

"Anywhere you want."

Elizabeth left her purse in the car. "Shirley? You called me about your horses?"

"That's right." Shirley Parker extended her hand. "Thank you for coming, Mrs. Murphy."

"Elizabeth, please. It's a pleasure. You mentioned on the phone they suddenly weren't getting along, after a year of seeming to?"

"That's right. They are both rescues, as I said, and were both show horses, although in different areas. Cap here," she went to the bay whose head hung over the top rail, "was a dressage horse, all pomp and circumstance, you know. And Missy, back there, was a ring horse, not the same at all."

Cap lipped and gnawed at Shirley's sleeve as

she stroked him. Shirley was smaller than Elizabeth by several inches, and looked well over twice Elizabeth's 28 years, though still bright-eyed and strong.

As Shirley spoke and expanded on her concerns, Elizabeth began to 'ground' herself, sending out mental roots and making sure her mind and spirit were clear to send and receive anything the animals might want to share with her.

Cap continued to dominate the physical space and Shirley's attention, but Elizabeth watched Missy, too. Missy was not happy with the attention Cap was getting. She distinctly said, *He is* always *first. He's always getting fussed over. I deserve that, too.* She stuck out lower lip and she rolled her brown eye.

She's no fun. She thinks she's a princess. She doesn't know how to have fun.

If Elizabeth had any doubt the speaker was Cap, he removed it by prancing in place, raising his hoof and waving it.

"Okay. I see what's going on."

"Yes?" Shirley asked.

"It's an ego thing. Missy is pretty strait-laced and came from a show background that Cap is working hard to diminish from his high up status as a dressage horse. Cap has a sense of humor. He knows it makes her mad to bring it up, so he does. He doesn't necessarily really believe that, but she's so easy to rile. Then Missy gets mad and retaliates by biting and chasing him. He comes off looking like the abused one, but it's mutual. Like siblings anywhere."

"I see. I can believe that. I've had Cap over 20 years, and Missy only one. The other problem is, Missy has started trying to do to me what she does to Cap. Now I understand why she does it to him, but how can I get her to stop doing it to me?"

"We have to come up with a plan and stick to it. Intermittent reinforcement is worse than none," Elizabeth said.

Shirley looked blank.

"If discipline is inconsistent, intermittent, the animal will continue the bad behavior indefinitely, because of the rare occasion that same behavior was rewarded."

"Ah."

Elizabeth explained further. "Now let me have a word with Missy. Without YOU butting in," she added to Cap.

Elizabeth closed her eyes and concentrated on Missy.

"Okay. I spoke to her and we resolved it. However, she has one condition."

"A condition?" Shirley repeated.

"Yes. She wants to be led from the paddock to the pasture first from now on."

Shirley smiled. "Of course. Missy wants to feel as cherished as Cap does."

"Exactly. I think you're on your way to a lovely relationship with Missy."

Elizabeth accepted Shirley's payment and said her thank yous and goodbyes to the horses. Missy was pleased with her day, but Cap had that rascally glint in his eye. Elizabeth thought she might get another call from Shirley someday.

As soon as she was out of the mountains and back in cell phone range, her voicemail rang. She pulled off the winding road and checked it. Tig sounding tense and worried. Please call his cell as soon as she got this message. She dialed.

"Tig, what is it?"

"Where are you?"

"On my way home. What's going on?"

"Terry's been hurt in a fire. I'm at the hospital with Janie." Terry's wife.

"Okay. I'll come too."

"Thank you."

Poor Tig. Terry Peterson was his best friend. Also a firefighter, Terry and Tig had been friends since high school. They had both made a ridiculous dare one night, after a few beverages, to apply to the fire department. They both got in, went through training, and were placed, although in different stations. They both got their college degrees while working as fire fighters, studying together and suffering together. They had even met Elizabeth and Janie around the same time, although in completely different circumstances. They had attended each other's weddings, and after almost five years of marriage, Janie was finally pregnant. Now this. It must be bad or Tig would have told her what Terry's condition was over the phone. The long grade into the city was seemed extra steep and to take forever. Finally she reached the hospital parking lot.

Emergency wasn't too busy on a Monday

17

morning and Elizabeth found Janie and Tig, along with several fire fighters still in filthy bunker gear, clumped in Waiting.

She hugged Janie and kissed Tig. "News?"

Janie clung to her hand and shook her head.

"Tig?"

Tig passed Janie to Macbeth, Terry's captain. Elizabeth thought he was a good man from the few times Tig had covered that station.

They walked a bit down the hall. Tig looked haggard. Elizabeth thought he had probably been awakened from a sound sleep. His routine was to breakfast with her, then when she left for her appointments, he slept until early afternoon. If he had a landscaping job, he tried to fit it in then, before he went back to work. Typically, after the 24 shift, he had three days off.

"Terry was coming out of a house fire, running out of air, and the floor collapsed. The house was under control, almost out really, and there was no danger... I mean, the house was a bungalow you know?" Elizabeth nodded. No basement. Who has a basement in California?

Tig's eyes were wet and his sentences disjointed as he tried to explain. "There shouldn't have been a hole. Or the floor shouldn't have collapsed. When Brian, Terry's partner, got out and he wasn't right behind him, Brian went back in. He was running out of air, too, but he just bolted in. Almost fell in the same hole. He saw Terry at the bottom, not deep, but the joists fell on him. He wasn't moving. Brian ran out of the house and got everybody going. Terry'd been out of air for a while, and he sustained some pretty bad injuries from the collapse." He ran a hand through his curls. "We're waiting for some news. They rushed him into surgery."

"Brian?"

"He's being treated for smoke inhalation and minor stuff, but he'll be okay."

The door to the ER pushed open and a doctor approached the group. Elizabeth and Tig joined them.

"Mrs. Peterson?" she asked. Janie nodded. "Can I have a moment?"

Janie said, "They are all here for Terry and me. You can say whatever you have to."

The doctor held her gaze for a moment then nodded. "He's got some pressure on the brain due to swelling from the head injury. He's broken a number of bones, including three ribs, left femur, and a cracked clavicle. His lungs are clear and he's responding to stimuli, so it looks good so far. We are draining the fluid from his brain."

Janie nodded. It looked like Captain Macbeth was the only thing holding her up. "When can I see him?"

"In a while. We're going to monitor him and I'll let you know. He'll be out for several more hours, though."

The unspoken news being *if Terry survived*.

One by one the fire fighters, already exhausted from the night before, slumped on waiting room chairs and slept. Janie managed to hang onto

Captain Macbeth and he let her. Tig and Elizabeth dozed. Patients and relatives came and went from the ER, but Terry's doctor did not appear.

Elizabeth was dreaming she was sleeping in a tree and could not get comfortable when Tig jiggled her. The doctor walked slowly down the hall, her dark features pasty with fatigue. Like dominoes, the party nudged itself awake.

Janie started to cry and the doctor held up her hands. "I think he's going to recover."

Janie cried harder. Macbeth spoke. "What's the scoop, doc?"

"Mr. Peterson had a drain installed and the pressure was removed," the doctor repeated. "The breaks and fractures will mend if he rests. He will need physical therapy for the femur; we had to put in a pin."

The fire fighters shifted and sighed. "Rest? That'll be the day," a voice mumbled and the tension left the group. "Janie never lets the boy rest," said another and Janie managed a weak laugh.

"Can I see him?" she asked.

"He's still in recovery, but I'll take you back." The doctor eyed the disheveled and worried group. "The bunch of you should go home and take it easy. Nothing you can do here."

"I don't know if we *can* take it easy," said an older woman so soot-covered only her eyes looked human.

"Well, for my sake, go take showers." The doctor smiled. "Mrs. Peterson? Follow me."

Elizabeth turned to Tig. "Wanna stay with

Janie?"

"Yes. Thank you." He hugged her tight. "I'll call you."

"I'll make sure you have something to eat." She kissed him firmly. "I'll feed Buster. Tell Janie." Buster was the Peterson's ancient pug dog who still thought he was a puppy. Terry and Janie lived across the street, so they pet sat for each other, too. For some reason, Teddy liked Buster. Probably pitied him, more like, Elizabeth thought fondly as she found her car and headed home.

Three

Elizabeth pulled into the drive, exhausted by the ordeal at the hospital. Teddy waited by the front door. He was often waiting for her when she arrived home. She used to think he heard her car and knew to come, but he even did it when she went for walks or came home in another vehicle. Now she believed it was her connection to Teddy. He "saw" her coming because in her mind, she pictured coming home. When she enquired about that, Teddy was inscrutably cat, his attitude *wouldn't you like to know?*

"Hi, Teddy." Elizabeth unlocked the front door and Teddy rushed ahead, tail waving. She was suddenly overwhelmed and sat on the moss green couch. Teddy, not a lap cat, jumped up to sit beside her, purring.

She petted him and mentally reviewed her day. Teddy head-butted her and kissed her hands when he could reach them. "So, Teddy, we're going to get Buster now and he's going to sleepover for a while."

Put my food up high, was his only comment.

Elizabeth sighed and struggled to her feet, the lure of the soft couch emphasizing how draining emotional trauma can be. She got the Peterson's spare key from the silverware drawer and crossed the street, Teddy accompanying her.

She sent mental messages to Buster telling him she and Teddy were coming and he would visit them for a while. As she unlocked the front door she heard his pet flap slap the frame and the click click of his paws as he tottered across the kitchen. Teddy rudely pushed in first.

You need some manners, Teddy, she scolded. Teddy ignored her and greeted Buster, nose to nose. Buster's eyesight was not very good, but his hearing was better and his nose perfect. Buster had been a shiny black pug in his day, but was now a mottled gray. Cataracts filmed his eyes. His bark was still youthful, although he didn't bark much anymore.

Elizabeth squatted awkwardly to pet him, and he stayed nose to nose with Teddy for several moments. She tuned into Teddy and got a series of pictures, fairly accurate from an animal's point of view. Teddy had never been to a human hospital, so he showed Buster pictures of the vet's clinic, with Terry on the tiny metal table instead of an animal. She had no idea how her mental pictures and descriptions were interpreted by Teddy, but apparently, he got the idea and filtered them so Buster could understand.

As Elizabeth watched, Buster got noticeably more agitated, so she sent calming energy to him and placed her hand on his back. *Feel my hand, Buster. It's okay.*

Daddy is hurt?

Yes, both she and Teddy responded. *But he's*

23

going to be okay. He has to stay at the doctor for a while, and you are coming to stay with us.

Like when they went on that trip?

Yes, just like that, Elizabeth reassured him.

Mommy?

Mom is fine. She's staying with Daddy.

Teddy butted in. *Come on let's go. I'll show you where mom buried a bird today.*

Buster shook like he was coming out of a bath and followed Teddy to the front door. Elizabeth gathered his food and water dishes, his new purple leash, then clicked on the small light over the stove.

At home, Buster did a perfunctory check to make sure nothing had changed since his last visit, which was yesterday when he and Janie had come over to discuss birthing options if Terry was at work when her water broke.

Teddy flopped in the middle of the kitchen floor, as much in the way as a rotund cat could be. Buster, satisfied, headed out the cat flap. A large cat and a small dog fit through the same flap and he knew his way around the yard. Elizabeth had explained to him early on where it was acceptable to do his business and by and large he respected that. Once in a while he lifted his leg on one lovely shrub or another and one day Elizabeth caught him.

What are you doing? We had a deal.

I can't help it. Racoon left a message and I have to answer it. It thinks this yard is okay to visit, and it's NOT!

Elizabeth had laughed and said, *Fine, as an exception, not a rule.* Buster lost interest and wandered away, his attention already on his next "message."

Elizabeth made a big pot of vegetable soup and took rolls out of the freezer to defrost. No word from Tig. Exhausted, she lay on the king-sized bed and fell instantly to sleep.

She awoke to darkness, a bit disoriented. Two lumps at her feet reassured her. Buster wasn't usully allowed on the bed, but somehow he had gotten his aging body up there, so Elizabeth let him lie.

The clock read 7:30 and she flipped on the bedside light. Her cell registered a voice mail message. Chagrined she had slept through it she confirmed it was from Tig. Only half an hour old, Tig reported Janie was being kept overnight at the hospital for the baby's sake, not that there was anything wrong, just the strain of it all. He would be home soon.

Elizabeth shifted her legs over the side of the bed and sat up, stretching. Teddy opened one eye, but didn't move. Buster snored on. He suddenly looked frail to Elizabeth, and she did a quick assessment. She didn't find anything new physically, so it must be the strain of his person in danger, she decided. She let him sleep and moved a step stool to the foot of the bed for him.

She took a quick shower and was toweling off when she heard Tig's key in the lock. She threw on her unsexy but snuggly pjs and met him in the kitchen. They hugged, not speaking for several moments.

25

"Hungry?" she asked.

"Starved."

"Sit and fill me in. I've got soup and bread."

"I'll just wash up." Tig went to the front bathroom while Elizabeth dished two bowls of fragrant soup and quickly nuked the rolls in a damp paper towel.

As they ate, Tig caught her up. "Terry's out of surgery and was responsive when I left. They let Janie go in right away and I hung around. They didn't like it, but eventually they let me peek in on him. Janie insisted. He looks pretty good for a guy who fell through the floor."

Elizabeth felt the relief coming off him in waves. "I'm so glad. How are you doing?"

"Good. Considering." He put his soup spoon down. "I talked to the guys from his station on that call, and it was kind of weird."

"What do you mean?"

"I don't know. Little things. His air ran out. A basement where none should exist?" He sighed.

"Haven't you run out of air?"

"Yes, but we have a low air warning buzzer, and we have time to get out of the structure. His buzzer malfunctioned. No warning."

"That happens, right?"

"Yeah. I guess. The basement thing, too, bothers me. Something about it isn't right."

"What are you thinking? Someone tampered with it?"

"I don't know." He buttered a roll and took a bite. "The call was anonymous, and by the time they got there, the house was fully involved. It was just a regular house, set apart from its neighbors, but when they got in, nothing was there. No furniture, I mean nothing. A shell. No one was around to ask about people in the house, so they knocked the fire down and then went in. It was all clear. Smoky but okay."

"Who told you this?"

"Brian. He was kind of in shock because he was one step ahead of Terry and he could have gone down the hole with him, or instead of him."

Their eyes met and they thought the same thing: Tig's call last night when the chief wanted Tig and his men to enter an unsafe structure and the roof promptly collapsed. So easy. So fast.

Elizabeth's heart raced as she saw how easily it could have been Tig in the hospital instead of Terry. She waiting to find out if her husband would recover. Her house empty and Teddy adrift.

She rose and took Tig's hand and led him to the bedroom. In silence and darkness they undressed each other and made love, holding on tightly as they sought release. Elizabeth's legs wrapped around her husband and she felt his heart beat strongly, reassuringly.

Some time in the night they moved apart and covered themselves. Elizabeth felt Teddy and Buster on the bed again, but didn't have the heart to move them. Tig snored comfortingly beside her and she gave thanks.

Four

Tig left coffee and a note. He had an early landscaping job but should be home for lunch. They could go to the hospital together in the afternoon.

Elizabeth took her coffee to her wicker chair and relaxed into her morning meditation. She was dimly aware of Buster snuffling in the kitchen and reassured him she'd take him for a walk in the outback.

She opened her eyes and wandered into the garden to check the koi. Teddy trailed after, Buster bringing up the rear. She tossed the fish some pellets and assessed them as they came to the surface to eat. They were so cute with their expressive faces and different barbles--whiskers--she like to call them. Like cats, a little. They had personalities and quirks. She had named them all and liked to think they knew their names, but fish weren't her specialty, so she really didn't know. Her readings on them were, well, *watery,* for lack of a better word.

Hey. Hey!

Elizabeth looked down and Buster's boogly, milky eyes appealed to her.

Breakfast?

"Yes, breakfast."

Treat?

"Yes, but you have your special diet first."

Ick.

"I know, but it's good for you."

Can't wait for that walk. I'm going to roll in something delicious!

"Thanks, Buster." She filled Buster's dish with his old-dog food, and Teddy's with fat-cat food, and checked her calendar. Ellen Fenwick's cats. Ellen was a big hearted lady who rescued cats and placed them in good homes. She ran her operation on a shoe-string budget out of her rural home and really did a community service. Elizabeth gave her a discount because she called so often. She sometimes did a phone consult, but had fun visiting. Ellen had a great sense of humor and Elizabeth enjoyed their relationship.

Hey. Hey!

Elizabeth recognized the voice and greeting immediately. Since Buster had begun to age, most of his conversations started with 'Hey.' Elizabeth thought it was because he was a little forgetful and just hoped *somebody* would respond.

"Yes, Buster, walkies. Let me dress." Elizabeth was a *Wallace and Gromit* fan and although she and Tig didn't have a dog, Teddy responded to 'walkies'.

Clad in jeans, sports shoes and a long-sleeved tee shirt labeled *Stag Bar, Lochdubh*, she went to the back door. Buster snuffled and gasped in his excitement and sat quivering in front of her so she could clip on his purple leash.

Buster had excellent manners, unlike Teddy,

29

and waited for her to lead him out the door to the back gate. Teddy pushed ahead onto the path that led to the trail. Buster was in ecstasy as they wandered at old Pug dog speed along the sandy path. Teddy accompanied them as usual. Elizabeth used to worry for him, since it was a well-used trail for hikers, joggers, horses and zillions of dogs. However, he proved capable of self-preservation on one walk when a large, aggressive, unleashed black lab had launched itself at him and gave chase. Elizabeth's heart was in her throat as tubby Teddy ran for his life. He scooted up a tree well ahead of the dog, and Elizabeth was filled with relief and anger. She never found the dog's owner. After that, she did stick to the trees when Teddy joined them on a walk.

The day was spectacular, clear and warm, the scents of summer in the air.

Elizabeth's cell phone rang and she checked before she answered. Tig.

"Hi."

"Hi. Whatcha doing?" he asked.

"Taking the guys for a walk. What's up?"

"Got a call from Macbeth." Terry and Brian's captain. "Preliminary investigation is arson, and I told you the basement thing was weird."

"What?"

"It was a slab house. Someone broke the concrete pad under the floor and dug a hole. It wasn't a real basement, just a hole. They covered it but it would for sure burn through."

"Wow. That's heavy duty."

"Yep. It could just be vandals, but it reads

30

like a set up to me."

"Yeah, a booby trap. For Terry?"

"They don't think so. Any fire fighter could have been in that house. Might not have been for us, but it's odd. A trap for someone, maybe."

Elizabeth knew the fire fighters were 'one.' What happened to one, happened to *us*. Sometimes it was confusing, when Tig wasn't on a particular call, but spoke as if he was.

"What about his air bottle?"

"Equipment malfunction. Didn't look tampered with. Points for Brian looking out for his partner."

"That's for sure."

"Okay, babe, just wanted to check in. Gotta go, my dirt's here. Love you."

"Love you, too."

Elizabeth took the 'guys' back to the house and grabbed her purse and a water bottle for her visit to Ellen Fenwick.

Five

Ellen Fenwick lived in a two bedroom, two bath frame house on a large plot of otherwise undeveloped land. Elizabeth pulled into the small drive, made smaller by trash cans, large animal cages and humane traps littering its borders.

Furry faces in the windows eyed her. She stepped carefully up the walk to avoid punting the greeter cats winding around her ankles. She didn't recognize any from her last visit.

She entered by the garage pedestrian door. The garage had been converted to a quarantine and hospital area with floor to ceiling cages and shelves. Everything was spotless and smelled faintly of bleach. She dipped the soles of her shoes in a tub with a thin layer of bleach water before she continued. One reason Ellen was successful was her commitment to germ warfare.

"Hi, Elizabeth." Ellen greeted her from the laundry tubs. She was a tall woman, sturdily built, short iron-gray hair capping a friendly face. Her blue work shirt, unbuttoned with the sleeves rolled up revealed the tee underneath that read "So Many Cats, So Little Time."

They hugged and Ellen guided her into the house.

"What have you got for me today?" Elizabeth asked.

Ellen paused to scritch various cats and kittens on the way through the house to a slider that opened onto the back yard. She shooed some potential escapees back gently with her foot and closed the glass door.

"It's a new rescue I just got yesterday. I actually called about another cat, but she was adopted so that problem is solved. Since you were scheduled, I decided to see what you think."

The yard was not large, but cat-proofed against diggers and jumpers. Within the space were several large outdoor cages and a stack of smaller cages against the house. Ellen approached one of those and slowly opened the door, making calming sounds. She pushed aside a towel draped for privacy and Elizabeth saw a tiny, big-eyed black kitten, poking out of white bandages.

"What's the story?" Elizabeth asked.

"Someone brought him to me. He was found at the site of a fire. He's badly burned and absolutely terrified. I took him to Dr. Knightly and got him checked out. I'm treating the burns here. If he does well, he can get his shots and things."

"He's so tiny," Elizabeth remarked. She sent calming waves out and the little guy stared, unblinking, back at her.

"Doc thinks he's about four weeks old. He's not bottle feeding, doesn't want me near him, but I think it's the burns not him, per se. He only eats if no one's around and the towel is closed. He probably feels pretty sick. I have to give him pain meds and I feel like such a bully."

"Hmmm." Elizabeth closed her eyes and asked the kitten permission to talk to him. He didn't respond negatively, so Elizabeth took it as yes.

Hi. I'm Elizabeth. Thank you for talking to me. How do you feel?

The response was slow and faint. *I hurt. I'm scared. Where am I?*

You are with the best person in the world to make you better. Her name is Ellen. Can you see or smell all the other cats?

Yes. They know I'm here and that scares me, too. So many.

Have they told you anything?

I haven't listened. I'm scared. It hurts.

Will you let Ellen help you?

Yes.

Can you tell me what happened to you? Elizabeth felt the kitten's energy wane. It was getting tired.

I was hiding. It got very hot and I couldn't breathe. My fur was melting.

Elizabeth got a picture of the kitten's fur curling and disappearing as the fire got closer. *Then what happened?*

I think I smelled air. I can't remember. I think I followed the air.

Elizabeth got another picture, this time of the kitten in what looked to be a crawl space under a house. It was in shock, but still managed to follow a draft of fresh air away from the fire. *You are a smart, brave kitty. Can I come back and talk to you another time?*

Yes.

Thank you. What is your name?

I don't have one. I'm tired. Sleep now.

Elizabeth redraped the towel and gently closed the cage. "Wow, that little guy's been through a lot. He wants to get better. He's not terribly feral, despite what he's been through. You're right, he's in a lot of pain and very scared, but he says he's willing to let you help him. He's really quite sweet."

Ellen nodded. "Do you have time for one more?"

"Sure."

"It's Betsey. She won't leave the birds alone. I don't know how she does it, but about once a week she gets one and leaves it by the slider door. I know it's a present, but she has to know I don't like it. She's a sassy one." Ellen led Elizabeth back through the house and out the front door to the ancient orchard near the drive.

Gnarled trees, sparsely leaved, extended to the main road some distance away.

"There she is, that rascal." Ellen pointed to an old apple tree. In its branches perched an enormous white cat.

"Yes, Betsey," murmured Elizabeth. "We meet again." She sent out her greeting to Betsey, who managed to look regal while awkwardly squatting in the tree.

Hello, Elizabeth.

How are you?

Excellent.

You know why I'm here.

I think so. Mom doesn't want her presents.

Do you have to kill birds?

Of course I do. I have to try. If you're going to ask silly questions, I'm not going to talk to you.

Okay. I'll make a deal with you. I won't tell your mom you can't help yourself, if you promise not to leave the birds where she can find them.

Why?

It upsets her. You love your mom, don't you?

Another silly question.

Well, she loves you, back. But the birds, you see, she loves them, too.

I love them, too.

Betsey!

I know. I know. It will make mom happy NOT to see them? I thought she liked presents?

Did she act like she liked them?

Well, no, but I thought she was kidding.

She's not.

Fine.

Elizabeth turned to Ellen. "I think we have reached an agreement. No birds." Elizabeth left it at that, but shot Betsey a look.

Fine!

"Wonderful!" Ellen said. "Would you like to stay for tea?"

"I'd love to, but I'm meeting Tig for lunch. Gotta get back."

"Oh, how is your handsome fireman?"

Elizabeth smiled. "He's fine, thanks."

36

They hugged goodbye.

When Elizabeth got home, Tig was in the shower. She fixed sandwiches and iced tea and set them on the patio table.

"How was Ellen?" Tig asked, his mouth full.

"Good. She says hello. How was the job?"

"Got my dirt in. Finish tomorrow."

He was so handsome, sometimes she wondered what he saw in her. She felt herself rather plain, pale freckled skin, gray eyes and wild brown hair. She wore little make up, but he acted as if she were the most beautiful creature on earth.

"What are you smiling at?" He had a smear of mayonnaise on his chin.

"You. I'm so lucky."

"I'm so lucky." It was an exchange they often had. A joke, but not really.

Lunch finished, they cleaned up and drove to the hospital.

Parking in the main lot was difficult, but they finally found a spot on the outer edge. Holding hands, they didn't talk as they found their way to Terry's new room. He'd been moved from ICU. Janie sat by his side.

"How's it going?" Tig leaned in to hug Terry. Elizabeth hugged Janie and then Terry.

"Pretty good. My head's pretty hard." Terry sounded weak, but like himself.

"I'll say." Tig pulled the visitors chairs closer and he and Elizabeth sat.

Elizabeth assessed Janie. She looked exhausted. "Hey, girl, you eaten anything?"

Janie looked surprised. "I, uh, don't remember."

Terry looked at her. "Hey, you better take care of yourself. How else are you going to take care of me?"

Janie laughed weakly. "Yeah, I guess. One baby at a time, right?"

"Hey, Elizabeth, take my wife out to lunch will ya? She won't leave me alone for a second. I wanna hear all about work since I've been gone. They can't do it without me, right Tig?" The smoke inhalation had roughened his voice. He reached for his water.

Elizabeth glanced at Tig and saw they wanted to be alone. Terry had something in mind. Tig nodded. "Yeah, Janie, give the poor guy a break. We've got man-stuff to discuss."

Elizabeth rose. "Come on Janie. I can tell when we're not wanted."

She urged Janie out the door. "Let's go across the street to the diner. I bet you've been eating out of vending machines, haven't you?" She saw the guilt flash across Janie's face. "You could live on Twinkies and chips back in the day, but you don't want that baby to, do you?"

Janie let herself be drawn across the street. They spent a pleasant hour before Janie wanted to go back.

"Okay, guys, time's up. Bonding over." Elizabeth came to Terry's bedside and gave him a resounding kiss on the forehead. "There you go. All better."

"Thanks, Elizabeth. I'll just check out now." Terry looked pale and tired, but his eyes had a bit of the old gleam.

They said their goodbyes and headed back to the car.

"Okay, spill. What's up?" Elizabeth asked.

"Terry wanted to catch up on the fire. I told him what I knew, and he went back over what he remembered. He also told me something interesting. Another arson in the north county had some similar aspects to his fire, and to my fire that same night. County Fire got called to a barn. Turned out nobody was in it. And again, it seemed stable, but the structure collapsed while the guys were checking it. No one was hurt but that was pretty lucky. I just think it's odd, three fires with injuries or potential injuries."

"What do you think?"

"I don't know what to think. I might take a drive out there tomorrow after I finish that landscape job. Wanna come?"

"You bet."

Six

The next day dawned beautifully, with a hint of summery warmth and wild sage in the air. Tig drove and Elizabeth watched the countryside roll by. At first they followed the same route she had taken to talk to the horses, but instead of turning off the rural highway, they continue further north to even windier roads bisecting large ranches.

The temperature rose noticeably as they drove further from the coast. Cattle grazed, tails swishing, on green hills. Tig turned onto a small road marked only with a hand-written number. After a few more minutes, they saw a burned out building leaning sadly toward the dirt road.

"That's it." Tig parked.

"Not much left," Elizabeth remarked as they approached the building.

"You're not going in," Tig said.

"WE'RE not going in," Elizabeth corrected.

"Right." He smiled at her. He circled the building and was lost to sight.

Elizabeth began her own investigation. She had already done her morning meditation, so she grounded herself again, sending her "roots" deep into the earth, asking for help from her spirit guides and making sure her energy channels were open and ready to receive. Sometimes it felt to Elizabeth like tuning in a radio station, ready to hear what was broadcast.

She picked up some scrabblings inside the building, perhaps from insects. Fire was decimating, but often the regeneration was remarkably fast; plants and insects among the first to explore a site.

She tried to connect with the bugs and 'see' inside, but that was not well-received and she got no helpful response. She hadn't worked with insects much. She found their energy interesting and completely unlike mammals or birds, or even fish. Still a work in progress, she thought wryly. She thanked them anyway, and 'moved' outside the building.

Birdsong filled the air. It had ceased when she and Tig arrived, but now it was back.

Hi everybody. She sent out a general greeting.

Hello hello hello hello came a wave of bright, happy thoughts.

I'm happy to see you today.

Happy happy happy! Much garbled chirping and fluttering, both physically and in their energy. As far as she could tell, they were mostly the same species of sparrow-like bird, but she did detect the more raucous voices of crows and whiskey jays.

Will you talk to me?

Talk talk talk!

Two nights ago, she projected two darknesses, two moon rises to them. They settled a bit, as if mimicking their nighttime behavior.

Yes yes yes?

Something started this, she projected the burnt out shell, *on fire.* She projected it burning.

Yes! Terrible! Frightening! A babble of flight and fear responses. She had to 'shout' to settle them.

One at a time! Who saw something?

Oh! I did.

Yes, what?

A lovely grub, so fat, and moving so slowly, so I---

No! About the fire.

Oh, that. No.

Elizabeth sighed. Her fault. Must be specific. *Did anyone see what started the fire?*

Who. A deeper voice.

You. Anyone.

Who.

Who saw what started the fire? Elizabeth felt a tad exasperated and ready to give up. Birds. Well, be fair, she scolded herself, some birds.

Who, came again.

Who is that? she called out.

A beautiful barn owl sailed past, wings outstretched. *It is I.*

Okay. Thank you, said Elizabeth. *Do you have something to add?*

Yes. Who.

I heard that. I don't understand.

The owl fluffed its feathers to suggest how dense she was. *It wasn't a what. It was a who. Who started the fire.*

Ooooohh. My apologies. While Owls weren't always as wise as they were depicted in literature, they were precise.

Did you see who, then?

Yes. Him. The owl flashed an image of Tig, coming around the building. Elizabeth opened her eyes, and yes, Tig was coming around the building toward the car.

What do you mean him?

I am clear.

But, it couldn't have been him.

It was.

All right. Show me exactly what you saw. She closed her eyes. The other birds were silent.

The owl showed her darkness, but a darkness unlike her own vision at night. It was clear and bright. She was inside the barn hunting. The sounds of rodents to the owl, were like the sounds of half-blind Buster crashing around the garden were to her. A human approached the barn and both owl and prey instantly stilled.

A man entered the barn, and true, he was dressed much like Tig today. What the owl clearly saw, was his ball cap with the word FIRE on it. The man moved about in the dark, and although the owl clearly saw it, its brain could not make sense of his actions to show Elizabeth. She got a series of random pictures. Suddenly the pungent smell of gasoline filled her nostrils and fire blazed up, silhouetting the man as he raced from the barn. She didn't often get smell with the communications, so this was extreme. The owl escaped through the dilapidated roof and the smaller animals dived for exit holes. From her point of view inside the owl, she flew to a tree some distance away and watched as the man got in a dark, boxy car and drove away.

Elizabeth felt the owl's fear of fire and of the man.

Thank you. Thank you very much. She sent soothing, calming waves.

You are welcome, was the solemn response.

She opened her eyes again to see Tig eyeing what was left of the front doorway.

"What did you find?" she asked him.

"Nothing the investigator didn't, I don't think. Accelerant, of course. Probably kids fooling around. The barn was clearly abandoned before the fire. The land has a grazing lease, nothing exciting there."

"Accelerant, yes. Kids, no."

In the five years they had been married, Tig had learned to trust her abilities. "What?"

"A man. Wearing a FIRE cap, just like yours."

"Hmmm. Why would an arsonist wear a FIRE cap?"

"Don't know yet. Fire fighter wanna be? Forgot he had it on? Thought no one saw him? Well, no ONE did."

"Won't be able to call *that* witness anyway." Tig smiled at her.

"Interesting that way out here, in this dry weather, the fire didn't total it."

"Funny you should mention that. Just so

happened County Fire was doing training a couple miles away and got called out just minutes after it started. Managed to save it from being totaled."

"Saved it, huh?" She smiled at the remains.

"Saved the woods, then."

Elizabeth saw how easily a major forest fire could have started. "Yeah."

They headed toward the car. "Do the investigators think it's related to the other fires, or this is a new guy?" Elizabeth asked.

"All the fires were the same night. Weird, but if the same guy started all three, he'd have to really make tracks to get to the different points in the county. This is an hour from the site of my fire and at least that far from Terry's."

"If so, somebody wanted you boys and girls busy."

"True."

Something told Elizabeth to visit the little fire kitten again. More to learn there.

Seven

After they got home from the north county barn fire site, Tig went off to a landscape job. Elizabeth called Ellen for permission to visit.

Things were much like her last visit: cats in the windows, greeter cats on the walk. Elizabeth went into the house through the garage again, stopping to bleach her shoes, and continued to the back yard.

Ellen waved hello from the far side where she was hosing out litter boxes.

Elizabeth undraped the 'security towel' and opened the kitten's cage. The same big eyes peered at her from the bandages. *Hi.*

Silence.

Will you talk to me?

Silence.

What's wrong? The kitten was trembling. *Are you in pain?*

Yes.

"Ellen? Did this little guy have his pain meds today?"

"Yes, but I had to take him to the vet for some debriding of his burns. It really hurts. They gave him a shot, too, but it's probably wearing off."

"Can he have more?"

"Let me get something else." Ellen returned with a needle-less syringe filled with liquid. "Here you go, honey." She expertly poked it into the side of the kitten's mouth and squirted before he could resist. "That will make him sleepy, so you'd better talk fast."

That should help, Elizabeth said.

Thank you. You are kind.

Will you talk to me about the night you got hurt?

I don't like that.

I know. I think it will help me figure some things out.

What?

I'm not sure yet. You were under a house when the fire started?

Yes.

Did you live in the house?

No. I lived under the house.

Why are you all alone? You are still little.

He showed her pictures of a car racing down a street and then him waiting under the house alone.

I'm sorry. Your mother lived there with you?

Yes.

What about brothers and sisters?

I don't know. I've always been alone.

A feral mom gives birth under a house, the other kittens didn't survive for whatever reason. Poor baby.

Did people live in the house?

I don't think so.

But people came to the house, yes?

47

Yes.

Can you show me what they did?

No.

But a series of noises filled Elizabeth's head and she realized if the kitten lived under the house, his view would be limited but he would be able to hear what went on. She heard a voice but words were indistinguishable. Heavy footsteps overhead. A huge noise filled the kitten with terror. He ran from his sanctuary to a shrub and waited, shaking, until night. She recognized the sound; a jack-hammer pounding the slab. Now she became confused. A concrete slab floor. The kitten lived under the house. How does that work? She asked the kitten to show her all of his area under the house. How he came and went, where the people, or person, went.

He showed her pictures of a sloping foundation. The front of the house was on a concrete slab and the back was on post and pier as the ground fell gently away. The whole house was surrounded by a wooden deck, hollow underneath. Whoever dug that hole in the foundation, deep enough for a person to fit into, definitely had something in mind. But what? Kidnapping. Murder. Nothing good, she though grimly.

Her thoughts returned to the present and found the kitten sound asleep, pain free at last.

An hour later at home, Tig eyed Elizabeth over the cage on the kitchen table. "Another cat? What will Teddy think?"

"I'm not sure yet. But he's so little. And so cute. He needs special care and I have more time

48

than Ellen does."

"You do?"

"Well. Sort of." Elizabeth pulled off the towel and showed Tig the sleeping bundle like a tiny kitten mummy. The bandages were loose to protect the burned tissue, but the effect was pathetic.

"Oh," was all Tig said. "A fire cat, for sure." Elizabeth had explained the kitten's injuries and circumstances at warp speed when Tig saw her pull the cage from the car. She had hoped he'd still be at the landscape job, but he had returned for more tools and caught her red-handed.

Tig was big hearted but more importantly, soft hearted. "What's Teddy going to think?" he repeated.

"Let me talk to him." Elizabeth found Teddy in the garden with Buster. Teddy in the sunshine, Buster in an adjacent patch of shade, both snoring contentedly.

Hi, Teddy. We have a new guest.

Who? Uncle Dave? He gives good belly rubs. Uncle Dave was Elizabeth's older brother.

No. A baby who needs your help. He got hurt in a fire and is pretty sick. I brought him home to get well. She sent pictures of the kitten to Teddy. She tried to make the kitten look very sad and needy.

Hmph. What do I have to do?

Nothing really. I have to feed him and give him medicine, but I was hoping you'd help me by watching him when I'm at work. I can't take care of him all by myself you know.

Let's go see this thing. Teddy stalked into the

49

house.

Elizabeth put the cage on the floor and let him sniff.

Pretty small. Will he live?

I think so. But he'll need a friend and someone to show him the rules and things. Could you help me, Teddy? He's very small and needs a... protector.

I'd be his protector?

Yes, Teddy. It's an important job and I can't always be there.

I suppose. The floor is cold.

Elizabeth smiled and rushed to get a fluffy towel for Teddy to lie on to watch the kitten.

Teddy? Where do you think I should put the cage, you know, later?

Teddy settled on the towel on his brisket, feet tucked neatly, tail wrapped around him, facing the kitten.

Probably my room, if I'm going to watch him properly.

Good idea. "Teddy's room" was actually the second bedroom, used as an office. Teddy almost never used "his room" because he liked to sleep with Elizabeth and Tig or on the living room couch. However, like most cats, he rotated his favorite spots and his room did make it into the rotation occasionally.

Tig had loaded his supplies and come to kiss Elizabeth good bye. He saw Teddy babysitting.

"Well, if Teddy thinks it's all right, I guess I do, too. You're not going to do this all the time, are you?"

"No. Don't worry. This guy is special. I can tell."

"They're all special to you."

"Yes, but not like him. And not like you. Have fun." She shooed him out the door and asked Buster if he wanted a walk. Teddy preferred to stay this time, but Buster was up and ready.

Eight

Elizabeth's day passed in a flurry of chores and errands, Teddy dutifully watching his charge. She fed the kitten, temporarily calling him Soot.

That's a stupid name. Teddy flopped to his side while she hand fed the kitten.

"I know. I have to call him something and I can't think of anything."

Well start thinking. It's really stupid.

It was difficult to feed him while touching him as little as possible. His wounds needed airing, his bandages changing. He was in constant pain and she worried about dehydration, finally inserting a subcutaneous liquid drip.

She continually 'chatted' to him, sending healing and calming energy. He was groggy, but purred.

I think you should leave his door open. In case I need to check on him.

"Remember, he's very delicate, Teddy. No playing or teasing."

I know. I can see him. Teddy was indignant.

Elizabeth complied and got stiffly to her feet. Her cell rang and she found it on the kitchen counter. Janie.

"Hi, Janie. How are you?"

"Good. Terry has turned a corner and I finally feel like I could go home."

"That's great. What about him going home?"

"Not for a few days yet. If he keeps doing this well, they'll take out the drain tomorrow and then we'll see."

"I'm so happy."

"Me, too. I wonder if you could pick me up? I feel like I can sleep in my own bed and I don't want to cab it."

"Of course, Janie! When?"

"They're bringing Terry's dinner so anytime really. I can't eat one more meal from the hospital cafeteria. After he eats they drug him up so he'll just fall asleep. He's starting to grumble about the baby and me, so I know he's better. I miss Buster and my own things, you know?"

"Sure, Janie. I'll be there in about half an hour, okay?"

"Call me from the parking lot and I'll come down. Don't go to the trouble of parking." She forestalled Elizabeth's protests. "You won't be able to see Terry anyway, so don't worry."

Elizabeth decided to take Buster since she wouldn't leave the car. Buster loved car rides, and when she told him they were getting mommy, he was beside himself.

She parked in the passenger loading zone and texted Janie. Buster panted excitedly, watching out the passenger window with bleary eyes.

The hospital doors whooshed open and Janie waddled toward the car, laden with bags and balloons. Elizabeth opened the rear door and helped Janie arrange her parcels. Buster wriggled until Janie settled herself in and buckled up. He gave up trying to lick her face around her abdomen, carefully tucked himself around her bulging belly and sighed.

"Terry's got so many plants and gifts in there you can hardly find him. I decided I'd better take a few of them home now. All the stuffed animals and most of the rest he's leaving in the children's ward." She rested her hand on Buster and Elizabeth didn't have to be a Reader to feel the comfort they gave each other.

Elizabeth pulled into Janie's drive. Janie unlocked the house and Buster raced inside to do a preliminary check.

Invaders! Came the cry from the house. Buster was in distress. *Invaders! Come quickly!*

"Stay here!" Elizabeth said to Janie as she ran inside. The three simultaneous fires, Terry injured, suspicious circumstances perhaps targeting a fire fighter, made her heart race.

What? Where? she called to Buster.

Here, in the kitchen!

Elizabeth envisioned the back door broken, a trail of blood or household treasures. Perhaps the burglar still inside. She found several cockroaches skittering from Buster's doggie door to the pantry door which was ajar. The roaches had found his bag of dog food and were making off with it, one crumb at a time. Poor Buster was traumatized.

"It's okay, Buster." She petted him.

It is NOT okay!

Elizabeth opened the pantry door further and moved the dog food.

"What's going on?" Janie called from the yard. "Can I come in or should I call 911?"

"Come in. It's fine." Elizabeth pulled a handful of food from the bag and took it out the back door, explaining to the cockroaches they must remain outside. She opened the back door.

If you don't, I can't guarantee the creatures who live here won't harm you.

She felt a sense of understanding and compliance. The roaches raced out the door and were lost to sight. She met Janie in the kitchen.

"Cockroaches, ugh."

"Shouldn't be a problem," Elizabeth said. "Could have been worse."

"I supposed. Jeez, I'm so tired."

"You go rest and I'll bring in the stuff. Call me later if you need help. Are you hungry? Want a sandwich or something?"

"Actually I am. I have some soup in the freezer."

"Let me nuke you a bowl. Go lie down. I'll bring it when it's ready, okay?"

Janie looked pale. "Yeah. Thanks. I'm about done in."

"I'll take care of Buster before I go. He'll want to rest with you."

Janie hugged her. "Thank you so much. You're a lifesaver."

Elizabeth found the soup and started it defrosting. She got a couple of bowls and filled one with water and one with food for Buster. He eyed it suspiciously.

"It's fine, Buster. I checked. Nobody in there. I'll bring your real bowls back tomorrow."

She unloaded the gifts and left them on the kitchen table, adding water to the plants. The microwave dinged and she took the bowl of soup to the bedroom. Janie was in the shower. She set the bowl on the nightstand. Buster was already on the bed.

"Soup's on, Janie. Sleep tight. Everything's done, so get some rest."

"Thanks again. See you tomorrow."

Elizabeth left the stove light on in the kitchen and made sure everything was locked up.

She drove her car across the street and was grateful to see the kitchen light on. Tig was home. The smell of Janie's soup reminded her she was starving. She wondered what she could produce for dinner.

"I'm home," she called from the doorway. Something smelled delicious. Bless Tig.

"Hey," he called.

"What's for dinner? I'm starved."

Tig came out of Teddy's room looking a little guilty. "Just checking on the baby."

"How's he doing?" She hugged and kissed him.

"Good. He ate a little canned food. I mixed it with warm water so it was soupy. He really liked it. He purred a little."

"Thank you. Teddy's quite taken with him.

I'm so hungry. Thank you for cooking."

"Just pasta and salad. Should be ready." He set about dishing up the food and she checked on the kitten.

How are you little guy?

Better. My brother is helping me.

Brother, huh? Elizabeth lay on the floor next to the cage and rubbed Teddy's belly. She scanned the kitten and found the pain somewhat diminished. His eyes seemed clearer, too.

"Dinner's ready," Tig called.

Okay, guys. I'll be back. Teddy, do you want me to put your food in here, too?

Sure, why not. He rolled over so his nose extended inside the cage. Soot pushed himself forward so their noses met.

Nine

Morning dawned cool and misty. It would burn off later, but now all was hushed in the neighborhood. Even the birds had decided to sleep in.

Elizabeth checked on Soot and Teddy. They slept next to each other, Soot in, Teddy outside of the cage. Tig had already left for his landscape job, but had made fresh coffee. She poured a cup and took it to her meditation chair.

So peaceful. So relaxed. So connected. She 'checked in' on Teddy: happy, snoring, getting hungry. Next she checked Soot: pain increasing, coming out of sleep, healing skin itchy, but content.

Elizabeth prepared meds and food and took them into Teddy's room. As she finished her animal care, her cell rang.

"Hi, hon." Tig.

"Hey, what's up?"

"How are the babies?" The family joke was that Teddy was their baby, but now they had two.

"Getting better all the time."

"Just letting you know, no landscaping today. Got a call and they're sending me over to Training Division for the new recruit class."

Training Division was a separate facility for

recruits, volunteers in training, and some refresher training for veteran fire fighters. It contained offices and classrooms, plus a large facility for climbing and running drills, myriad scenarios to practice.

"For how long?"

"At least a week while we work with the fresh meat. Just their last bit before graduation."

"Are you there now? So, day shift?

"Yep."

"Thanks for letting me know."

"Gotta run. Love you."

"Love you, too."

Elizabeth changed into jeans and a tee. Teddy decided he could leave his charge for a while and he crossed the street with Elizabeth. She knocked on Janie's door. Janie opened the door looking rested and very bulbous.

Elizabeth hugged her. "You're gonna pop any minute now."

"I wish. I still have four weeks, if you can believe it. I haven't seen my feet for months, and this kid's working out on my kidneys." The baby was now feet up, able to pummel Janie's innards at will. "I'm having tea, want some?"

"Nope. Peet's." Elizabeth referred to her favorite brand of coffee. "How are you doing?"

"Good. Better. Nice to sleep in my own bed. I just told myself Terry was working."

"Good for you. Need a ride to the hospital?"

"Nope. I can drive, but thanks."

"Need any errands done? Chores?"

Janie eased into a straight-backed chair. "No,

I'm fine. Really. I'm going to visit Terry, then maybe stop at the store. If my feet let me. I'll be back in time for a nap."

"All right then. But call me if you tire out. I'm going to the store anyway; it's no trouble to pick up a few things for you." Elizabeth wasn't going to the store anyway, but was sure Janie over estimated her stamina.

The morning passed quickly and Elizabeth returned home for lunch.

Soot was calling. He looked bright-eyed and comparatively active. The three-inch lip of the cage door was too much for his wobbly legs, but he wanted out. She gently lifted him over and set him down. He stood spraddle-legged like a new calf while Teddy sniffed him thoroughly.

Ick. Hurt. Medicine. Teddy's assessment.

Elizabeth sent a picture to Soot of her taking off his bandages. Where they stuck to him, she knew there would be pain, so she dosed him with his pain meds first. He was resigned to the process.

When she finished, she was in worse shape than Soot. Sweat beaded her brow and muscles trembled from the exquisite care she had taken. He, on the other hand, purred and stayed still as an angel, the only sign he was hurting was a wince or a slight break in his purring.

Do you want to stay out of the cage now? she asked Soot.

No. I like it. Can you make it so I can get out though?

Yes. I'll fix it. Elizabeth thought about it and

finally made a small ramp on both sides of the lip with towels. *How's that?*

Soot wobbled back inside on his own. *Good. Tired. Sleep.*

Teddy came back during the ramping procedure. *I'll watch him. You can go.* He dismissed her.

She laughed and kissed him on the head. He squinched up his eyes and purred.

Elizabeth took a quick shower and was deciding what to wear when she saw Tig's clean uniforms hanging on his side of the closet. After several days off, he sometimes forgot to take fresh uniforms.

She would drop them off at Training Division. It was out of the way on the other side of the city, but it was a lovely day for a drive. Her cell rang. Tig.

"I'm bringing your uniforms."

"How did you know I was calling about that?" She didn't answer. "Never mind. It's still kinda creepy sometimes. You know that, right?"

"Yep. But I promise to use my powers for good instead of evil. Be there in an hour. Bye."

"'Kay. Bye."

The drive was uneventful, the rolling hills of their little town gave way to the city, and then appeared again on the other side as she neared the training facility.

She parked in back and saw a recruit class drilling. An aerial truck had positioned its ladder and the look on their faces was priceless as the instructor indicated they were to go up 100 feet.

Tig wasn't in the group so she entered the main building and went to the offices. "Excuse me, I'm looking for Tig Murphy?" she asked of a fire fighter manning phones.

"Don't know him."

"Okay. Where are the guys who arrived this morning?"

"Classroom."

"Where is that?" Elizabeth was getting impatient with his rudeness. He wasn't overwhelmed with paperwork and ringing phones.

"Out the back door to the building across the yard."

"Gosh, thank you so much." Sarcasm was lost on him.

She re-crossed the yard as a fearful recruit went up a few more rungs. The ladder swayed and he was only half way.

She shivered in empathy. She hated heights unless she was in the view point of a bird. *I could never get up that ladder.* Her admiration for her husband rose.

Entering the building she found a long hall with classroom doors on both sides. Following the sound of voices she peeked in an open door. Rows of occupied school desks filled the room. A fire fighter lectured at the board and Tig sat opposite the door, waiting for his turn. He saw her right away and circled behind the recruits and out the second door.

"I brought your uniforms but left them in the car 'til I found you. How's it going?

"About as boring as expected. We have some good ones, I think, but time will tell. A bunch of them won't even make it through the class, much less get hired. There's a couple real prizes in there."

"Isn't it too early to tell? I mean, didn't you just get them this morning?"

"I can tell." They walked to the parking area.

"Any news about Terry?"

"Could be coming home at the end of the week."

"Great news." She handed him his clean uniforms. "Why don't you show me where you stash your stuff in case I have to bring you something else."

"Good idea. That way I can spend a little more time with my wife, too. I'll give you the nickel tour."

Back in the main building, they went to the living complex. First, a common room, unoccupied at this hour, with large screen TV, couches and chairs, books and magazines, a kitchen and dining area, and stairs she thought led to the sleeping quarters.

Lockers were in a room adjacent to the kitchen, which could also be reached directly from the engine bay. A piece of masking tape with *Murphy* scrawled on it marked his locker. He punched a number on the electronic lock. "It's your birthday," he whispered in her ear. "Want to see upstairs? Where the beds are?" He leered at her.

Elizabeth laughed. "If you have time. Don't you have to teach or do something?"

"Something. Later we're breaking into cars."

"Burglary?" she joked.

"Jaws of Life."

"Ah."

Tig led her upstairs to several large rooms lined with beds, and a few closed doors. "Grunt sleeping quarters." He pointed to the closed doors. "Captain's sleeping quarters."

"I couldn't sleep with all the snoring. One guy snoring is enough for me."

"Very funny. You get used to it though, and usually you're so tired." They went back downstairs to the engine floor, which separated the living quarters from the offices. The trucks were gorgeous, huge and shiny. All the gear on the floor was immaculate and neatly stowed.

At the offices, Tig whispered, "This guy's an asshole."

"I know," she whispered back.

Tig threw open the door so it bounced against the wall, startling the heavy set young man. "Joey! How are you?"

"Jeez, Murphy. Like to give me a heart attack?"

"I want you to meet my wife, Elizabeth."

He didn't look at her. "Nicetameetcha."

"It's a real pleasure, Joey." She looked around the office as she listened to Tig chat with Joey. She recognized her husband's false tone as he irritated the man under the pretense of hearty male bonding.

A notice on the board caught her eye. A

temporary position was available in the office. The pay was pretty good and she'd be near Tig. Have to see if he thought that would be a good idea. Some travel, taking documents from station to station, so maybe not totally boring. Her work with animals paid well, but could be unreliable in terms of regularity. She occasionally took odd jobs for extra money. Tig said she didn't have to, but he worked landscaping *and* in the fire department. She wanted to contribute more.

She turned her attention back to Tig who slapped Joey on the back, just a tad too hard.

"'Kay, Joey, you take care of yourself now." Tig held the door open for her and walked her back toward the parking area.

"There is something weird about that boy," Elizabeth said. "Does he hate women, or what?"

"He's got a bad attitude. He's in the office as a punishment. He fainted after trying to go up the aerial ladder, collapsed right in the captain's arms. He almost got dropped from the class, but they're giving him another chance. He's got to start this section over again. I think they hoped he'd quit."

"Good luck with him."

"Thanks. What's your day like?" He leaned into the car to kiss her.

"Janie. Terry. Soot."

"What soot?"

"The new baby. I didn't know what else to call him."

"Right. Have a good day, then. Should be home for dinner."

"Oh, I saw a notice for some temp work in the office here. Would you mind?"

"Course not. Nice to have you around, but you know you don't have to."

"I know. I want to. It's only a few weeks while they are doing some paperwork archive thing. I'd be shuffling documents from station to station, or storage or something. The notice said something about converting paper to digital storage. Pay's good if I don't get bored to death."

"Sure thing. Gotta go." One more kiss and he sprinted across the yard toward the classrooms.

Elizabeth decided to go home and apply after she did her animal care. She could hear Soot fussing for food and attention when she focused on him. Teddy was doing his best, but Soot needed her.

Ten

After Elizabeth took care of Soot and Teddy, she left them cuddling in Teddy's room. She flipped open her laptop and went to the website she'd jotted down. Through a complicated search of the city site, she finally found the job application, filled it out and submitted it.

After a quick sandwich, she crossed the street to Janie's, and rang the bell.

"Hey, Janie, it's me."

The door opened. "Hi, come on in. Tea?"

"Sure." They went to the brightly lit kitchen where water was already on the boil. Elizabeth assessed Janie.

"You're looking good. How do you feel?"

"Enormous, but good." She poured hot water into the pot to steep.

"How are the feet?"

"I wouldn't know; haven't seen 'em." Janie laughed. "Pretty good. They hurt if I stand or walk too much, but they haven't swelled up as much as I thought they might." She eased into a chair and sighed.

"What's up with Terry? I was going to visit him today."

"Good news. He's coming home tomorrow."

Janie's smile was radiant. "I had to swear that you would be here to help me take care of him before they'd let me bring him home. Was that okay?"

"Sure. Of course. I would be here anyway, you know that." Elizabeth got a swift picture of a little boy with red-blond hair and freckles. Her mouth involuntarily made a big O.

"What? What?" said Janie.

Janie and Terry had made the decision not to know the baby's sex. Elizabeth didn't really read people. Animals were her area, so the little boy popping into her brain was a surprise. She didn't want to give it away.

"I, uh, think maybe the baby might arrive early, that's all."

"You saw something didn't you!"

"Just that it might come sooner than your due date." Elizabeth fumbled trying not to reveal what she had seen.

"What's wrong? Why?"

"Nothing. I swear. Everything's fine. It just sort of flashed."

Janie poured tea into two mugs. "You'd tell me, right?"

"Of course. If I thought something was wrong I'd drag you to the hospital to check."

"Okay. Wanna visit Terry with me?"

"Are you sure? I was going to visit him today, but I don't want to interfere."

"I'd love for you to come. He's so crabby. That's probably why they're getting rid of him. I think he's well enough to come home, based on his complaining alone." Janie sipped her tea. "I am so relieved. When he just lay there I was so scared, Elizabeth. Now that he's bitching about the bandages, and 'my ass hanging out,' that's a quote by the way, I just want to hug him and not let go."

Elizabeth laughed and pictured Terry, buns flapping, running the hospital staff ragged.

"When do you want to go? Did you eat this morning?"

"Yes, mom, I did. Are you free now?"

"No problem. How about I drive? Then I can let you off at the door and park?"

"You're a saint."

"Nope, just feeling sorry for you."

"Thanks. I've got to change and feed Buster. Half hour?"

"I'll be back." Elizabeth let herself out and crossed the street.

When she opened her front door, her cell rang. Tig. "Hey, miss me already?"

"Of course, but that's not why I'm calling." She heard the smile in his voice. "I happened to mention you were interested in the clerk job and they want you to interview today, if possible. Apparently, no one has applied for this fabulous position and they're desperate to find a body."

"Thanks. I'm so flattered, I'll rush right over."

Tig laughed.

"I'm taking Janie to the hospital to visit Terry. Can I come after?"

"Probably. Call the office and let them know

you'll be down. They'll be thrilled."

"I bet."

"No, they will. Maybe we'll both be done at the same time. How 'bout I take a hot file clerk out to dinner?"

"If you can't find one, can I go?"

"Love you, bye."

"I'll call you later and let you know what's up. Bye."

Elizabeth stopped in Teddy's room. Both cats were asleep, Soot curled into Teddy. His bandages were cleaner and drier every day, and his course of anti-biotics was nearly over. He was even growing some new fur. The fevers had stopped and his appetite had improved. His ears had been burned so they had a crinkly appearance that made him look like a gremlin more than a cat. The vet had said time would tell what the ears would be like. His hearing didn't seem to be affected, however.

They were so cute sleeping. She couldn't resist. She lay on the carpet and petted both. Soot with one finger on his forehead, and Teddy all along his back just the way he liked it. They both opened their eyes but didn't move.

Hi, mom.

Hi, mom. A little echo.

Hi, guys. Hungry?

I could eat. Teddy could always eat.

Not right now, Soot said.

I'm going to visit with Auntie Janie for a while.

Is Buster coming over?

70

I don't think so. Not yet. Maybe when Soot's bigger.

About that name, mom. I watched something on the box with dad, about this guy who climbs walls like a spider.

Teddy told me about it and I like that. I used to climb a lot. Can my name be Spider?

Um, I am not sure daddy would like a cat named Spider. He's not too into spiders because he meets so many in his work. Can you think of something else?

Teddy sighed. *I guess we'll watch more on that box and see.*

Okay. Soot was amicable.

Elizabeth grabbed her purse and phone and went to pick up Janie.

At the hospital, Terry was just as advertised, looking strong, relatively healthy, with the disposition of a feral cat. They stayed an hour, joking and talking about what he would do on his time off before he returned to ride a desk at work. The Fire Department wouldn't let Terry resume any kind of duty for at least a week, and then only after medical cleared him with that broken femur.

Elizabeth pecked him good-bye and gathered up another armload of flowers to take to Children's. Janie's kiss was much more enthusiastic.

"Hey you guys, get a room, jeez."

They broke the kiss. "I can't wait 'til you're home," Janie said.

"Me, too." Terry still held her hand.

"For Pete's sake, between her giant stomach

71

and your injuries, do you think you might give it rest?" Elizabeth joked.

"No," they both said.

Janie picked up the rest of the flowers to be donated. "I'll bring you clean clothes tomorrow. What time they kicking you?"

"Just like a hotel. If I'm not out by noon, they charge me for another day."

"I'll call you early."

"You better."

Elizabeth and Janie stopped on the Children's floor. Bright murals of forests and fairies decorated the hall. At the nurses' station they were directed to set their gifts on the long counter. The nurses would take care of them. Part of Elizabeth felt relieved and part felt guilty.

"I don't want to see these kids," Janie whispered. "Not now, not when I'm pregnant."

"I know. I'm sorry. Let's go."

In the elevator Janie said, "I didn't think it would be so hard. I didn't think about it at all until we were there."

"Don't worry. Your baby is fine."

"You're sure?"

"Yes."

"I want to go home. I'm tired."

Elizabeth saw how the visit to the Children's floor had disturbed Janie and sent her calming energy as she brought the car to the entrance.

"I don't feel too good." Janie heaved herself into the passenger seat.

"I'll get you tucked in with Buster and some

tea, how's that?"

"Sounds good."

When they pulled into Janie's drive, she looked pale. Elizabeth helped her into the house and to bed, eased off her shoes and covered her warmly. For the last couple months Janie'd had to rest on her left side, so she faced the bedroom door. Elizabeth pulled a chair over to the bed.

"I'll be right back with some tea." She felt Janie's forehead. No fever.

In the kitchen she started tea water and fed Buster a few kibbles.

What's going on with Mom?

She's tired. You know the baby is coming soon, right?

Yes.

She needs your help, you know.

I know. I help her every day. I exercise her.

Elizabeth laughed. *You sure do. I have an appointment later. Will you stay with her while she sleeps?*

I always do.

Your daddy comes home tomorrow. Elizabeth sent Buster a picture of Terry in the hospital bed, looking well and happy.

Buster's nails clicked on the linoleum as he did a dance.

Okay, I'm taking tea to your mom. You come, too.

Yes yes yes, coming!

Elizabeth sat in the bedside chair and put the tea on the nightstand. "How are you doing?" Buster jumped up beside Janie.

"Better. I was just tired. Overwhelmed a little, I guess. I've been keeping it together for Terry, and now that he's coming home, I'm just exhausted. The Children's floor was a surprise. I wasn't ready for it."

Elizabeth handed her the mug. "I didn't expect it either. Should I call your doctor? What's it like in there?" Elizabeth always asked this, referring to the baby.

"All's quiet on the western front."

"Want me to wait until you fall asleep?"

"No, Buster will do that."

"That's true. All right. I'm just across the street and a phone call away. Where's your cell?"

"In my purse I think."

"Okay, I'll get it and leave it next to you. That way you have two phones in an emergency." Elizabeth brought Janie's whole purse to her. "Just in case," she added. "I'm going down to the Training Division to interview for a temp job pushing paper. I can be back here in a flash, if you need me. I won't call until dinner time or so. Don't want to wake you."

"Thanks, Elizabeth."

"No problem." She made sure the burners were off in the kitchen and the front door was locked.

Traffic was easy before quitting time. Half an hour later she pulled into the Training Division lot where she had parked a few hours ago. No one was in the yard now, but otherwise it seemed the same.

In the office, Joey had been replaced by a young woman fire fighter.

"Hello. I'm Elizabeth Murphy. I have an appointment to interview for the temporary clerk position."

"Boy am I glad to see you," the woman said. "Nobody applied and I've been doing it all. Please take it!"

Elizabeth laughed. "I probably will."

"I'll tell them you're here. I'm Denise McGill. I go by Denny."

Denise exited through a side door.
Moments later a captain Elizabeth didn't know shook her hand.

"Thanks for coming. I'm Bob Hutchins. Come on back." He led the way and she followed to a small conference room where a woman in street clothes was already seated.

"This is Connie Duchamp, our administrative liaison from Human Resources. She'll be sitting in on the interview." Captain Hutchins sat behind the table.

"Nice to meet you. I'm Elizabeth Murphy." Elizabeth extended her hand and received a firm shake from Connie.

Elizabeth sat in the only other chair. Connie watched her closely as if she were a suspect. A quick glance told Elizabeth Connie was the one making the decision. Connie's short silver hair was neat and business like. Her stocky figure sat erect, hands folded on the table over a stack of files. Sharp blue eyes, no glasses. Fine wrinkles put her age at about 50.

"Connie, would you like to start?" asked the

captain.

"The job lasts approximately three to four weeks while we play catch up. It consists of filing, data entry, some driving throughout the county, and probably a lot more I can't begin to describe now." Her voice had begun to thaw. "It is basically 9 to 5, not much in the way of evenings or weekends, as it now stands. That could change. You'll be based here, at the Training Division. No benefits. Questions?"

"I, uh, don't know what to ask."

"Can you type on a word processor?"

"Yes."

"That's all you need to know right now. Can you come in tomorrow to start training?"

"What time? I'm supposed to help Terry Peterson's wife check him out of the hospital in the morning."

"Ah. Terry, sweet boy." Connie seemed fond of him. That was something. "Come at one then."

"Yes, thank you. I'll be here." They both thanked her for coming and she found her way out, realizing the captain had added nothing to the interview.

On the apparatus floor, she wondered where to look for Tig. Probably the classrooms, since that was why he was here. She crossed the yard to the class complex. She didn't hear any classes in progress, but walked down the hall to check. Maybe he was doing paperwork in a classroom.

The building seemed empty until she got to the other end. She heard muted voices from a room with a door left ajar.

"It's your attitude that's holding you back." She recognized Tig's voice.

"It's *their* attitude. I have experience, but no one cares about that."

"What experience?"

"Um. You know. I read a lot. I've been in this training as long as the others."

"And now you're getting supplemental training."

"I don't need supplemental training. And I don't need to be in the office doing fucking secretarial work with the girls. I do fire." Elizabeth recognized Joey's voice.

"You do fire?"

"Shut up, man."

"I'm cutting you slack, but I'm still senior to you, and one of your instructors. Watch your mouth."

A mumbled response. Elizabeth didn't want to be lurking in the hall when Joey came out. She hurried out an exit to the yard. Moments later Joey stormed out the same door. She was caught by surprise, since this side opened onto an empty lot. No buildings, cars, parking, nothing. He ignored her and stomped down a faint trail at the bottom of the lot.

She found Tig in the classroom gathering his materials. "That Joey's something, isn't he?"

"You caught some of that?"

"Sorry, I wasn't eves-dropping. I was looking for you. I waited outside when I realized what was going on."

"He's got a real chip. Like he's better than the guys who've been on the job already. Hungry?"

"Starved."

They walked to the parking lot together. "Where to?"

"Green Stuff."

"You got it." Green Stuff was Elizabeth's favorite restaurant; an all you can eat soup and salad bar. Tig liked it too. The breads and desserts were incredible.

Eleven

The next morning passed quickly for Elizabeth. Meditation, animal care, taking Janie to the hospital to check Terry out. He looked tired but relieved to be coming home. She got them settled and they both looked like they needed a nap. Buster was beside himself.

Tig was long at work, so Elizabeth grabbed some lunch and drove to the Training Division to start her own training. She hoped Joey wouldn't be with her on her first day. He wasn't.

"Elizabeth!" Denny rushed to hug her like an old friend. "I'm so glad to see you. Let's start over here." She indicated a stack of files a foot high. "What we're doing is putting them chronologically into the data base. It's easier if we do it together."

The rest of the afternoon passed quickly and they completed the files by five.

"That wasn't so bad." Elizabeth stretched.

"Come with me." Denny led her to the next office and showed her a stack of file boxes head high.

"Oh, my God. We're not doing all that, are we?"

"Not all. Some will be burned, some stay just the way they are, but a lot of it is us, yes."

"Oh, boy."

"Now do you know why I was so happy to see you?" Denny closed and locked the door.

"Now I know why no one applied."

Denny laughed. "See you tomorrow. We'll finish that same section of files and then we switch to old personnel files. I think we sift out the 'retireds' and 'deads.'"

"Sounds fun."

Tig was waiting at her car. "How did it go?"

"Fine. Boring, but at least I didn't see Joey all day. Denny is great."

"Yeah, I like her. Really hard-working and dependable. Joey was working on his aerial ladder skills. He can't even fake it. He about had a heart attack again."

"I'd be exactly the same. It freaks me out to think of you wobbling around at the top of that toothpick ladder."

"It doesn't thrill me either, but at least I can pretend." He kissed her. "Home?"

"Yup. See you there."

At home, they made dinner together and shared some wine. Teddy joined them at the table.

Mom, Spider wants to come out. Can he?

Sure.

A few moments later, Elizabeth said, "Tig, look."

The tiny black kitten wobbled out and sat next to Teddy.

"He's so cute," said Tig. The kitten's eyes still dominated his face. Elizabeth had left his bandages off and he looked positively miniscule with little fur to fluff. "Is he in pain?"

Are you in pain? Elizabeth checked in.

No. Feel pretty good.

Can we pet you?

Maybe a little chin scratch would be nice.

"Tig, try scratching him under the chin."

"Are you sure?"

"Go ahead."

Tig used one rough finger to scratch gently.

Aaaahhh.

"He likes you, Tig."

"I can't believe how small he is."

"Speaking of wounds, I helped Terry come home today."

"How's he doing?"

"They both looked beat, but coming home is good, you know?"

"Yeah. Maybe we can have them over for dinner tomorrow."

"I'll see if they're up to it. What's happening with your training class?"

"Got some guys from County Fire in. Talking about rural fire fighting. Told us there's a new arsonist setting fires along the highway. Small grass fires, easily put out, but it's getting warmer now. Fire season's coming. It won't be so easy to put them out in a month or so if they don't catch him."

"Any leads?"

"They think he's throwing prepped matchbooks from a moving car. They take a few minutes to light an area big enough to see. By then, the guy's far away."

"I thought arsonists like to see their work?"

"They do. We're not sure where he goes to watch, though."

"Why isn't it in the paper?"

"It will be. Trying to keep it out as long as possible. Don't want to feed his ego."

"This seems like a lot of fires in our area."

"It is. Something's up, but we don't know what it is. They're having a meeting with the arson team at work tomorrow--with reps from all the departments county wide."

"Sounds big."

"I think it is. Lunch tomorrow?"

"Sure, what time?"

"A little late, I think. Oneish?"

"You know where to find me."

"I sure, hey." Tig looked down to find the small black kitten clinging to his jeans clad calf. "Okay little guy, up you go."

He gently pried the claws free and set the kitten in his lap. "This okay?" he asked both Elizabeth and the kitten.

Elizabeth checked. "Okay."

The kitten curled up into an impossibly small ball and purred, eyes adoringly on Tig.

"Somebody's got a kitten," Elizabeth teased. "Stay there, I'll clean up."

They made an early night of it, tucking in the cats and themselves in their respective beds.

Twelve

The next day passed much as the day before. Elizabeth reported to Denny, Tig to his students. They met for lunch. Elizabeth had packed a picnic lunch. The Training Division lot backed up to the hills, with trails to myriad scenic outlooks. They didn't have time for a hike, so parked themselves at a ratty picnic table on a rise that overlooked the Division and the town beyond.

Elizabeth unpacked and they ate ravenously of chicken sandwiches, sundried tomato hummus and pita chips, seedless grapes and iced tea.

"I made junk food cookies, too," Elizabeth said, referring to her chocolate chip cookies with macadamia nuts, dried cranberries, and this time, coconut shreds.

"Almost good for you!" Tig answered in their standard joke. "When did you have time?" He bit into a giant cookie and moaned with pleasure.

"I made them a couple days ago and froze them for emergencies." Elizabeth worked on her own giant cookie. "I consider being potentially bored to death an emergency."

"So, how's it going in data entry? People treating you okay?"

"I'm mostly being ignored, which is fine by me. Denny's great. Maybe we can have her and her boyfriend over for dinner one night?" She made it a question because Tig knew more background on the people he worked with, and although he might enjoy them at work, that didn't mean he wanted to socialize outside.

"Sure. I think she dates a guy in insurance. Lenny? Benny? Something like that. I thought it was funny because their names rhymed.

"John Tenny. Yeah, he's in insurance. They met when he was investigating an arson for his company and needed info. He likes skiing and tennis and is allergic to beach sand."

"Beach sand? Boy, you don't mess around. How long did you grill her?"

Elizabeth laughed. "We have a lot of time to talk, and once we get going, my brain doesn't need to do anything but copy data."

"Okay, explain a beach sand allergy."

"Well, not the sand really. A fungus is in the sand at certain times of the year, so he can't go to the beach. Especially when it's windy."

"That is so weird."

"It's not just the beach sand, either. It just sounds funny to say that. The fungus is in a lot of areas in this county. So many people have allergies in the windy season. Everything is just blown around."

"I know. Half the guys are sneezing and their eyes are running. I'm glad I don't have allergies."

"Me, too." Elizabeth packed up the stuff

going home and Tig took the trash.

"Back to the trenches," Tig said.

They walked back to the main buildings, kissed and parted ways.

Elizabeth sighed resignedly at the thought of another three plus hours stuck at a computer. She had just sat down when Denny returned.

"You are so lucky!" Denny said. "You're busting out of here."

"What do you mean?"

"Document transfer, Bay Station. Your neck of the woods. WE need some stuff brought here, but I am SO wonderful, I talked them into letting you bring them back with you tomorrow."

"Why didn't you take it? I mean, that was really nice of you, Denny."

"I am a wonderful person. Besides, I'm doing another pick up right near John's office." She smirked and waggled her eyebrows.

"Okay, I feel better. I thought for a second you were too nice to be real. Ulterior motives, I get." They knuckle bumped and laughed.

"Okay, we gotta do, what, an hour and half more here, and then we can bolt for the day. Wheee!" Denny did a funny rock-dance, thrusting her hips in and out.

Elizabeth's laugh burst out loud and abrupt.

"What? I'm just skiing!"

Elizabeth texted Tig her change in itinerary and drove to Bay Station.

She pulled into the small sloping parking lot and went into the office.

85

A clean-shaven middle-aged fire fighter glanced up from a computer. "Can I help you?"

"Yes, I'm Elizabeth Murphy from the Training Division. I'm supposed to collect a box of files."

"Sure. Hang on a sec." He clicked his mouse a few times and rose. "I'll just go get the captain."

He returned a few moments later with a round-faced man in a captain's uniform. She tried not to stare at his hair plugs. So NOT natural-looking.

"I'm Captain Jensen. You're looking for some documents?"

Elizabeth again explained her mission. "They didn't call?"

"No. But don't worry, they'll be here somewhere." He turned to the other man. "Wanna call and find out exactly what she needs?"

Elizabeth stood awkwardly in the middle of the office.

"Do you want to come back?" Captain Jensen asked.

"No. I'm supposed to wait for them. They need them first thing tomorrow."

"It might take a while.   Have a seat."

Elizabeth inwardly groaned. Just what she needed at the end of the day. Instead of getting home early, she'd probably get home late.   She texted Tig to let him know. She pulled her pocket calendar from her purse and checked her appointments for next week. She'd have to change a dentist appointment due to her new job. She didn't like going to the dentist, so no big deal there. She pulled out old gum wrappers, tissue, and an ancient throat lozenge and threw them all in a waste basket. The office was quiet while both men were out looking for her materials. At least she hoped they were.

She got drowsy, but was so uncomfortable in the office chair, she kept shifting her position. She decided to check in with Teddy and Soot.

Teddy was hungry. Of course. Wanted to know when she was coming home. She sent him a picture of herself waiting in the office. He knew she couldn't come home, but didn't know why, since to him, she was just sitting in a chair. She tried to equate it with a picture of Teddy waiting by a pocket-gopher hole.

Ah. He got it. He probably thought she'd bring her catch home with her, but she'd explain later. After all, he didn't always catch what he waited for. Soot was sleeping. She felt for pain and got just a slight throbbing where he lay on his side. He still couldn't really curl up cat-style because of his healing tissue, but he was much more comfortable. She sent him warm energy and in his sleeping state he began to purr.

A box hitting the desk stirred her out of her trance.

"Dozing, were you?" The first fire fighter had returned with a document box.

She blinked up at him. "Not really." She saw he didn't believe her, but she didn't care. "Did you get through to the Training Division okay?"

"Sure. They want our reports from 3 to 5

years ago for input into the computer."

"Hard to believe they are still not on."

"I know. We are *so* last century."

That sounded so odd coming from this older man that Elizabeth couldn't hold back a laugh.

"I have a teenage daughter. Sorry, it just slips out sometimes."

"That's great. Okay. Just the one box?"

"Oh, no. It's just the one I could grab. Where are you parked?" He saw the dismay in Elizabeth's face. "Don't worry, the guys will take them out for you."

"Oh. Thank you."

"It's not too bad. This is just fire reports. I have three times this in medical calls. Division said they wanted them all. Something about a central data base for the county. It's about time. Right now all our stuff is separate, so cross-checking is really hard. We have to call each station and ask the right person. Makes it hard to share information." He picked up the box and indicated the door.

"You sure know a lot about it." Elizabeth led him to her car.

"I've been doing this a long time. I'm the one who bugged Division to do this. I'm not their favorite because of it. It's pointless in this day and age not to be able to access other stations. I mean, the state data base is more up to speed on recent stuff, but you have to hop scotch around to compare data."

Elizabeth unlocked her trunk. "Should I move my car closer to where the records are?"

"Sure. Move your car in front of the office

88

and I'll get some guys to bring the rest."

"Thank you so much for all your help."

"No problem."

The rest of the boxes were loaded. Elizabeth drove the few blocks home accompanied by Teddy's rumbling in her head that he was starving to death, despite a bowl of cat food sitting in his room.

Thirteen

Tig pulled into the drive just after Elizabeth. By the time she had unlocked the front door, Teddy was waiting inside, ready to lead her to the kitchen. Soot wobbled behind him.

Well, where is it? Teddy demanded.

What? Elizabeth asked.

My gopher. I've been looking forward to it. It's not dead already is it? You know I like a little life left.

It got away.

Figures. What's for dinner?

Kibble for you, and baby food for the baby.

What's the point of getting up anymore? He flopped, belly up, on the kitchen floor.

Elizabeth bent and gave him a full massage. "Poor baby."

Tig opened the refrigerator and stared. "Nothing really."

"You mean nothing you want to cook."

"Yup. You?"

"Nope."

"Pizza?"

"Pizza."

"Greek veggie? I'll call."

"Thanks." She gave him a kiss and went back to her car. She didn't feel right about leaving sensitive documents in her car overnight, even in this safe neighborhood. The boxes weren't too heavy and there were just four of them. She set the first inside the front door. She'd have to load them up again in the morning.

"Let me help." Tig followed her out and grabbed two boxes. Elizabeth got the last one, the one with all the fire reports. As she crossed the threshold, the bottom fell out of the box, scattering paper everywhere.

"Crap. Just what I need. Now I can spend the evening sorting and refiling this instead of something important, like watching videos with my family."

"I'll help. Let's put everything on the table. We can sort it out over pizza, okay?" Tig hugged her. "It's okay."

"I'm just so tired. That was stupid. I should have checked the box first."

"It's okay. I'll help you sort. So will Teddy." That got a smile from Elizabeth. Teddy really liked to lie down in the middle of any perceived action, whether it was the kitchen floor, the bedroom floor or a work area strewn with documents. Teddy particularly liked tax season, when he could be counted on to make an appearance.

Elizabeth started making piles, leaving the middle of the table clear for the pizza box. She had just finished picking up the reports from the floor when a racing engine drew her attention.

91

"Pizza's here," she called. Tig met the delivery at the door and brought in a fragrant box.

"Let's just use paper tonight, okay?" He set the box on the table and brought in paper plates and napkins. "What do you want to drink?"

"Water, please." Elizabeth washed her hands and returned to the table as Tig set a glass of water at her place and a beer at his own.

"Smells great." She grabbed a slice and bit in, long strings of cheese trailing.

A few slices of pizza later, the world looked a little better. She pulled a report to her and checked the filing date.

"What do you think? By date or by event? How do you guys file?" she asked.

"Both. I mean they are supposed to be cross-referenced, but that's your new job, right?"

"Right. Okay, so since I'll end up doing this anyway, let's do it by date and if it's an arson, put it here," she indicated a small hole in the debris, "and if it's an accident, put it here." She pushed aside another mound.

"What if it was never determined?"

"Here. And I'll start a log of the report numbers so if I'm doing it wrong, I can fix it easily."

"Easily?" Tig smiled.

"Well, sort of." She smiled back.

For a time they sorted in silence, only interrupted when Tig rose to get another beer and Elizabeth put the pizza things on the kitchen counter.

"Hey," she asked. "Do you notice anything?"

"I notice my back hurts and I haven't really

92

made a dent."

"Me neither." They surveyed their small piles of progress. "What I mean is, I'm noticing my fires, all my fires happened around the same dates. Whether they were found to be arsons, accidents or undetermined, they seem to be in clusters. Here, look."

She pulled her piles to her and read off the dates. "It doesn't happen all the time, but a lot of the time. We don't have a lot of fires here in the Bay district, so maybe it was never noticed, but look."

"You're right. Over a period of a couple days, we'll have some action, and then nothing for a while. Then more clusters. But the fires are so different, they weren't compared. Or if they were, they weren't determined to be related."

"And since this information isn't in any sort of comprehensive data base, no one thought anything of it. Well, I suppose the way it's written up, even then, it might not have been noticed."

Tig pulled several reports to him. "Look at this. Just these three are very similar to what's happened this week all over the county." He read her the details. "An abandoned house in the country, a house fire and a warehouse. All of these have strange circumstances. I mean, roofs falling in aren't uncommon, but with close calls to the fire fighters, it seems odd. In each case, someone's life was put at risk. More than usual."

"Do you think we're reading more into this than is there?"

"I hope so, but I have a feeling." Tig had been

with the fire department for eight years. Elizabeth trusted his feelings. They had saved his life more than once.

"I'm wiped out." Elizabeth realized how tired she was. She tuned in to Teddy and Soot, both complaining at the lack of attention they were being paid.

"Me, too. But I'm going to look into this."

"When I go in tomorrow I have to input these reports. I'll see if I can find out more about the other stations' reports, too. I know they all won't be in the system because that's what they hired me to do, but I might be able to get somewhere since I know what I'm looking for. These only go back three to five years. I can go to the other stations if I have to and get more stuff."

"Just be careful. You have access to all that, but you don't want to raise any flags. Let me know right away what you find out. Don't tell anyone else. You are an employee now so it's logical for you to find out things. One thing you can do is keep a list of arson suspects the reports eventually led to, if any. You'll have to dig into subsequent reports, which these records don't reflect. Maybe we can get some solid evidence if this really leads somewhere. If it doesn't, I don't want to say anything and be embarrassed."

"I know. The last thing we want is to jeopardize your shot at Captain." Tig had been thinking about taking a run at the next Captain's exam. If he made Captain, it meant a pay bump and a bit more stability as well as responsibility. They had talked about it-- that it would also signal the green light for starting a family.

"You take the first shower." Elizabeth went back to the reports.

"Let me tape that box for you." Tig rummaged for duct tape and secured the box.

"Thanks." Elizabeth gave him a kiss. "Now go. Teddy wants the bed warmed up for him."

Tig laughed and headed to the bedroom. Teddy and Soot trailed behind.

Elizabeth put the papers in order for later reference.

Something about this bothered her, but she couldn't pinpoint it. Bad enough someone was setting fires that seemed to endanger the fire fighters more than usual. She felt in her gut this was related to the three fires that had occurred this week. Terry falling in a basement of sorts, the house in the north county, Tig's warehouse fire. A pattern was forming. It had started years ago, but no one had noticed. Why on earth would anyone do something like this? She hoped it was her overactive imagination.

The shower shut off and Elizabeth went to take her turn.

Fourteen

Elizabeth and Tig woke at the same time, blearily drank coffee and readied for their respective days.

Elizabeth had not slept well, unable to get her mind off the sinister aspects of the reports. Even as she slept, she tried to file and refile, making empty explanations of the results, but her subconscious would not let her come to any positive resolution. It ended by throwing all the papers on the floor again and she gave up sleep about the same time as Tig.

"Should we drive in together?" she asked. "Do you have anything special going on?"

"I don't think so, but you never know. I guess we could risk it." His smile lit up his face. It always made Elizabeth smile, too.

They loaded his car this time and Tig drove. The way to Division was long and convoluted. 'You can't get there from here' accurately described the journey. The streets followed the hills. Instead of a grid pattern the way was curvy and indirect. It could be frustrating if one was in a hurry.

"Lunch?" she asked.

"I don't know. I'll text you. I don't know what's on the schedule today. More classroom stuff I think."

"Okay. I'll get some office types to bring in

these boxes. I don't know where they want them."

They parted with a promise to keep in touch and Elizabeth made her way to the office. No one was there so she turned on her computer and decided to do a little research. Not technically her job, but what the heck.

First she used a search engine for arson and got a jillion hits. That would not be helpful. She next gave some parameters for dates and unsolved. That was better. However, if the pattern she and Tig had thought she'd found was correct, this wouldn't help either. It was a non-pattern pattern and very smart. Very hard to track. Accident, arson, some solved some not. What if some of those solved, weren't really solved? What if they were set up? Or known arsonists were charged when they hadn't done it? Sheesh. No way of knowing that. And a criminal case. Where would she find that? This was going to be a lot harder than she thought.

The door opened and Denny breezed in. "Morning!"

"Morning," Elizabeth said. "Somebody's in a good mood."

"*Somebody* had a great evening!" Denny winked.

"I'm glad. Hey, where should those boxes go that I picked up from Bay Station?"

"Good question. Let me ask." Denny whipped out the door and Elizabeth was left alone again.

The door opened and slammed shut. "Oh, it's you." Joey, the recruit on probation, or punishment, or whatever, glowered at her.

"Yes. It's me." Elizabeth didn't feel overly friendly anyway this morning, and Joey just about topped it off.

"Where's the coffee?" he asked.

"Where did you leave it?" she asked politely. The look on his face was priceless. She stifled a laugh and concentrated on her computer screen.

He stomped over to the coffee maker and slammed around making a pot. Elizabeth prayed for Denny's quick return. Joey sat at the phone desk and pulled out a newspaper. It was clear he would be no help with records today.

Denny came in. "We can use an empty classroom for now. We're going to get lots more records, faster than we can input them. The good news is we only do fire reports, not medical. That's for some other poor slob later." She looked over at Joey just as he looked up.

"Don't look at me, Blondie," he said. "I ain't doing shit."

"I'm not and no kidding," Denny answered. Elizabeth and Denny laughed because clearly, she *was* looking at him, and he was not doing anything. Also, Denny was not blonde.

"No help there," Elizabeth said. "Let's go." The women left the office and crossed the apparatus floor to the lounge area, where several fire fighters on break watched the news and drank coffee. "Hey, guys," Denny asked, "Can we get some help?"

"Sure," came some answering grunts. "What do you need?"

"Couple boxes moved to a classroom."

"What's in it for us?"

Denny started to answer but Elizabeth cut her off. "Cookies. Homemade cookies."

"I'd do anything for a cookie," said an older man, whose pot belly was nicely formed.

"We know, Andy," Denny said.

Elizabeth led the way to Tig's car and unlocked it with her key. They sometimes needed to trade vehicles.

They each grabbed a box and Elizabeth found the bag of leftover junk food cookies she'd given to Tig.

Denise had a key to Classroom 4 and they stashed three of the boxes there. Elizabeth tried to carry the box of fire reports back to the office, but Andy insisted on taking it.

"I said I'd do anything for a cookie, and I meant it," Andy said.

"Well, thank you. You can have two." Elizabeth handed him the bag of cookies after he set the box on her desk.

Joey eyed the bag of cookies, but Andy ignored him and retreated to the TV room.

"Okay, what first?" Elizabeth asked Denny. "These new ones from Bay Station?"

"Sure, might as well." Denny pulled up a new data base and showed Elizabeth how to enter data so it could be cross referenced. The data base was different from the one she had used yesterday. Not only did it take forever to fill in the appropriate windows, Elizabeth made many mistakes and had to back track and make corrections. By lunch time she was so frustrated she knew she had to get out for a bit.

She told Denny she leaving and texted Tig she was going for a walk. He texted back immediately asking if she wanted lunch. She did. They met at the picnic table. He brought food from the Division cafeteria. Not fantastic, but fine in a pinch.

Tig saw her face and said, "You go first. How was your morning?"

She filled him in and added that Joey had done nothing all morning except take a few phone calls, most of which he let people in other offices answer.

"This data base was designed by a chimp! If you don't enter it in exactly the right way, it moves the info down a window. Then you can't back it up a window, you have to re-enter the whole thing. I could just scream. It will be a miracle if anyone can find anything on the computer."

They finished eating. "Walk?" Tig asked.

"Absolutely." They set off down the little trail at the end of the lot.

Tig was silent for a few moments. "So, you're doing older report data, right?"

"Yes."

"So, newer cases should already be input, right?"

"Should is the operative word," she said grumpily.

"I did a little digging of my own in between

100

trainings."

"And?"

"I couldn't find anything."

"Big surprise."

"No, but now I'm thinking. What if the data were entered incorrectly. You said how easy it was to make a mistake. Maybe that's why I couldn't find anything."

"I looked too, and didn't find anything. But that was before Denny taught me how to use the data base. Anyone looking up data would know how to use it. Like you."

"Yes, I know how to look up reports. But I didn't find anything. So maybe, we need to look it up 'wrong.'"

"Maybe." They walked on, silently, holding hands, each lost in his own thoughts.

They reached a rise that overlooked the valley. Division was below and to the left. Lovely.

"I feel better. Thank you." Elizabeth squeezed his hand.

"Just doing my job, ma'am."

"I smell a fire," Tig said.

"Probably just someone's barbeque or fireplace."

"No. That's a house fire." He started down the hill through the brush, pulling out his cell phone and dialing.

They rounded another rise and saw a cul-de-sac of moderate homes, one of which was on fire. Tig reported it as they ran.

"I'm going in." The side of the blazing house

was near a fence and tall landscaping. The second floor windows had burst and flames flicked out toward the trees.

Elizabeth heard a dog whining and opened the side gate as Tig, after trying the front door, climbed the fence to a deck and pulled himself to the second story,

The yard was filling with smoke and toward the back, a black and white shape moved back and forth uncertainly. The smoke became more intense and Elizabeth dropped down on hands and knees and called to the dog.

Hey, come here. I'm going to help you.
I can't. It's bad. I'm scared. It smells.
I have to take you out. It's not safe.

No, don't. Elizabeth made her way to the frightened dog. She took off her jacket and threw it over its head, then picked it up and ran for the street. The dog weighed about 40 pounds, but Elizabeth was so wound up it seemed to weigh nothing.

Sirens came closer and as she reached the far side of the street it was suddenly clogged with trucks, men, hoses and neighbors.

She didn't see Tig, so she sat on the sidewalk cradling the dog.

Are you hurt?
No.
Was anyone else in the house?
No. Everyone was gone. Just like every day.
What happened? Did you see anyone?
Man. Strange man. Went inside.
How do you know?

102

I could smell him outside the gate. Then he went into the house. I heard the door open. He was inside for a few minutes and I smelled smoke. You came right away.

Where is he now? Elizabeth removed her jacket from the dog and let it look around. She noticed a collar and dog tag. Doodle. *And Teddy thinks Soot is a silly name.*

No. He's not here.

Should I call the number on your tag? Just then Tig found them. He bent down and hugged her.

"I was getting a little worried when I didn't see you."

"We're okay. This is Doodle. She says a man went into the house just before it caught fire. She didn't see him, she heard him. Says she doesn't know him, so probably not the owner. She's got a phone number on her collar. Should we call it?"

"I will. It needs to be official."

"Can they save the house?"

"No, but they can save the neighbors'. Best we can do."

Elizabeth glanced at her watch. "Oh, my God, I'm so late."

"I'm sure you'll be okay. You're on duty. Doodle rescue."

"What do we do about her?"

"I'll call the owners. In the meantime, see if any of the neighbors will watch her. Gotta check in and then get back." Tig left her and she watched him talk to the Captain in charge.

Elizabeth pulled out her cell phone and told

103

Denny to tell whoever was in charge of her—was it Connie in H.R. or Captain Hutchins? She didn't know—why she was late back from lunch.

Denny laughed. "Hey, no problem. Everyone ran like a bat out of hell down there. Everybody loves a good fire! Even Joey disappeared right after you went to lunch."

Elizabeth explained her Doodle rescue and said she would be back after she found someone to watch the dog.

"Okee doke. I'm just here twiddling my thumbs. Now that Fetal Boy isn't even on phones, I'm doing that, too."

Elizabeth rose, bent at the waist, holding Doodle's collar. She wished she had something to make a leash so she wouldn't have to walk like that. Tig, as usual, read her mind, jogged over with a piece of line and tied it to Doodle.

She smiled in thanks.

"What?" he asked.

"You have a big smudge across your nose," she said.

"You're no prize yourself," he pointed at the front of her blouse coated in Doodle fur, dirt and ash that had floated down from the second story.

"Wow," she said. She brushed at her hair and a snow storm of ash followed. "Well, I feel pretty."

"You look amazing." She probably looked amazingly horrible, but she knew he really thought she looked lovely. "You did good." He hugged her.

"Doodle!" A little girl of about ten ran over with her mother. "Thank you for saving her!"

"You're welcome. I'm so glad you're here. Doodle was worried and I was just going to look for a neighbor to watch her for you."

Elizabeth eased away and let the Captain talk to the mother and daughter. Daughter clung to Doodle who leaned against her legs.

Elizabeth didn't see Tig so she started back up to the trail. She had no idea how to get back to Division from this street. Only half an hour walk by trail. She texted Tig on the way.

Head down, arms churning, she marched up the hill through the brush. Her head filled with thoughts of data entry and fires set perhaps with murder in mind, she didn't see the snake until she was two steps from it.

First she saw the triangular head and shock stopped her immediately. Next she noticed it was dark brown, an unusual color for the area. It lay straight and still as a stick, partially in the trail. She would have stepped on it in two seconds. Her heart sped up and her stomach felt queasy with adrenaline as her eyes followed several feet of snake to the eight rattles on its tail.

She backed up a couple steps trying to calculate how fast it could coil and how far it could strike. She had a quick image of the snake launching itself at her like it was catapulted. *That can't happen.* She hoped.

Hey, guy. I'm not going to hurt you. Could she go around the head-end of the snake and continue without upsetting it? Or her. No answer. She calmed herself, no easy feat, and sent out waves of harmlessness--or what passed for that--while her heart raced and her hands shook. The snake didn't move.

I just want to go past you, okay? I don't want to hurt you. And I don't want you to hurt me.

She looked the snake in the eye. Were you supposed to do that? Not to dogs, that was a threat. Cats it was okay. She had no idea about snakes, and this one was giving her nothing. It watched her, looked relaxed, not moving, not seeming threatened. Who knew? She was good at reading most animals, even was getting the hang of insects a little, but snakes were not her area.

I'm just going to walk on by, nice and slow, buddy, okay?

She took a tentative step forward. It took all her courage not to run. She stepped evenly and carefully as far to the right of the snake as she could. She watched him out of the corner of her eye. Didn't want to make eye contact in case that was a NO in snake-dom.

The snake didn't move and Elizabeth speed walked her fastest mile ever back to the Division lot and the picnic table.

She burst into the office and startled Denny.

"Holy crap!" was Denny's greeting.

"Snake." Elizabeth panted.

"What? Where?"

Elizabeth caught Denny up on the fire and snake adventure.

"So, what should I do now? It's almost four. I can do an hour."

"I guess you haven't looked at yourself lately." Denny stood with hands on hips. "Come with me."

"I know I'm a little smoky, but you guys should be used to that by now." Elizabeth protested on the way to the ladies locker room.

Denny shoved her in front of the mirror.

"Holy crap is right," Elizabeth agreed. Her hair was gray with ash. She looked about 70. Smudges and lines of soot streaked her face. Her clothing was filthy and covered with Doodle hair. She had left her jacket at the scene. She felt stinky, not only with fire, but the sour smell of fear sweat, thanks mostly to the snake. Just thinking about it made her heart speed up a little.

"I don't have anything to change into, even if I was prepared to shower. I guess being a clerk is a dangerous job here."

Elizabeth decided to keep a change of clothes and a shower kit in her car like Tig did. He had his home station, but was sometimes sent to other stations with little notice and so kept emergency supplies in his car.

"Captain's not here, so I'm in charge. I love saying that. Anyway, everyone's down at the fire scene and won't be back today. Go home; you're disgusting." Denny smiled.

"Thanks. I feel disgusting. Oh, shoot. Tig and I rode in together." She checked her cell phone. Tig had texted back he would be doing paperwork and would cadge a ride later. Just as well. She really didn't feel like hanging around in her present condition.

She clocked out, got an old beach towel from her car's trunk and laid it across the seat. She surveyed herself and wondered if it was worthwhile to try and save her clothes. She really liked these jeans and the teal blouse. Her jacket. Rats. She liked that, too. She texted Tig to see if he could find it and bring it home. *Good luck with that.*

The drive home was painfully slow at rush hour. All the lights were red, all the drivers stupid. She sighed and sent a message to Teddy.

Hey, guys. I'm on my way. Everything okay, there?

Teddy's energy pulsed with excitement. *We're good.*

How's Soot?

Soot's gone! Teddy was ecstatic.

Oh, no! What happened? Where is he?

We watched the box, Mom! He's Edward now!

Elizabeth was completely lost. She knew the box was TV, but how could they be watching it? She must be overtired.

Okay, is Edward, who used to be Soot, okay?

He's fine, Mom. He's sleeping. Home soon, home soon!

That was Teddy's refrain when she was on her way. He seemed to know when she would arrive and it always caught her off guard. She was on the long stretch of fertile farmland between the city and their cute little beach town. Traffic moved along well and she was only minutes from the driveway.

Yes, home soon.

All she wanted to do was shower and lie down. Dinner. Agh. Another problem perhaps solved in the freezer. At any rate, to be tackled later. Much later.

Fifteen

Elizabeth could barely get her key in the front door she was so tired. She staggered directly to the bedroom and dropped her purse. Sure enough, Teddy and Soot, um, Edward, were together on the bed, and the TV was blaring.

What's going on? Why is the box on? How is the box on?

I turned it on, Mom! Look!

Teddy lay on the remote, which had been left on the bed. It was on the movie channel Tig was fond of.

Okay. Can you turn it off, Smartypants?

Are you mad at me?

Elizabeth was suddenly contrite. *No, Teddy. It's fine. I'm tired.*

You smell awful.

I know. I'm going to shower and you can tell me about Edward. Elizabeth turned the TV off and moved the remote to Tig's nightstand.

After her shower she felt much better, but no less tired. She put her smelly clothes in the laundry room and returned to the bedroom.

She lay on the bed and Teddy immediately came up to be scratched. Edward slept on, but she rubbed his forehead with one finger. The fur was growing back nicely, in patches.

Teddy snuggled by her side. Not much of a lap cat, he liked to be within scratching distance.

Okay, tell me about Edward's new name.

I turned the box on and we watched a story about a person with claws, just like us!

Elizabeth imagined werewolves or something, but when she tuned into Teddy, she saw Edward Scissorhands. *We liked that story and Edward has long claws, too. He can't pull them back all the way, so they get caught in things just like that man. Edward liked him so he said that was his name. I said it was okay. It's okay, right?*

Sure, Teddy. Whatever you guys want. Elizabeth was sleepy. Aches surfaced in muscles she didn't know she had. She pulled up the comforter and let go.

The muted ringing of her cell phone dragged her out of sleep. She groped on her nightstand where she usually kept it. Not there. Farther away. The room was dark. That was weird. She turned on the light and saw her purse on the floor, the ringing emanating from it.

Tig. "I'm sorry I'm so late. I'm on my way. Need anything?"

"No, thanks. I'll dig in the freezer and see what I can defrost for dinner if that's okay."

"Sure. Home in a few. You all right?"

"Just groggy. Fell asleep after I got home."

"Okay. Bye."

"K, bye."

Elizabeth padded to the kitchen and checked the freezer. Chili and rolls. Sounded good. She set the container of chili in the microwave and preheated the oven for the rolls.

Time for Edward's anti-biotics. He was almost done with them. He was healing so nicely.

In the bedroom, she didn't want to startle Edward by just grabbing him and shoving a pill down his throat, so she gently called to him.

Edward? His limbs twitched in a dream. She wasn't good at entering others' dream states, but it was good practice. *Edward?* She concentrated and let his dream enter her mind. He was in a dark place, but it was very hot. Smoke curled around him. He was afraid.

Edward? It's okay. You can wake up. Mom's here.

Edward twitched and cried out, trying to run from the smoke. It quickly turned to flame. She felt his fur begin to burn. He ran, encouraging the flames to burn more fiercely. He escaped from the dark under a house. He shot into a hedge which scraped the flames out. Her heart raced with his and she lay her hand on his flailing limbs, slowly bringing him to the surface and safety.

Edward. It's okay. You're safe.

His eyes opened wide and his breathing slowed as he recognized his surroundings. He began to purr and she explained about his pill. He took it with good grace.

"Tomorrow's your last day for pills." She kissed both cats and rose as she heard Tig's key in the lock.

She greeted him in the kitchen with a kiss. He

had managed to shower at the station and he looked presentable. Well, actually, fantastic. She gave him a hard hug.

"What?"

"I missed you, that's all." She released him, put the rolls in the oven and started the chili again in the microwave.

Elizabeth dished up the food and they caught each other up on events after the fire. She told him about the snake and Edward's new name.

"Teddy and Eddy!" He laughed.

Edward. Not Eddy. Elizabeth recognized the little black cat's voice.

Yeah, Teddy echoed. *Eddy and Teddy is stupid.*

Stupid is your new word, Teddy, Elizabeth scolded.

It's a good word. Useful. Teddy rolled on his back next to her chair.

"Ai!" Tig exclaimed. He reached down and picked Edward off his jeans' leg and set him in his lap.

"Edward prefers to be called Edward. Not Eddy," Elizabeth said solemnly.

"Message received. I hope he grows out of the leg climbing thing before he gets much bigger."

"I'm pretty sure he will if you call him Edward." Elizabeth rose to clear the dishes.

"The Scissorhands part is sure accurate." Tig stroked the tiny cat with one strong finger.

Elizabeth felt contentment pouring from all three of them in the dining room. She smiled and

113

continued to clean the kitchen.

Her cell rang from the counter just as she hung up the dish towel.

Janie's cell number. "Hey, I was thinking about you."

"Well, I'm starting labor, that's probably why."

"Aren't you early? Why are you so calm? Where's Terry?"

"What do you want me to say first?" Janie sounded giddy.

"Do you need a ride to the hospital?"

"No, Terry's driving me. At least it was his left leg he broke. I'm early but still in my target range. I'm fine!" She forestalled the worry. "I just wanted to let you know. Will you watch Buster?"

"Of course. Should we come?"

"No. They won't let you in, only Terry. I don't know how long this labor will be, but I'll call you when I know more. Gotta go, Terry's got the car out. We're off!"

Elizabeth hung up. "We're gonna be aunt and uncle soon."

Later she and Tig lay in their bed, Edward and Teddy on each side of them like bookends.

"Exciting, huh?" Elizabeth linked her fingers through his.

"Yeah."

"Don't tell them, but it's a boy."

"How do you know? The doc tell you?"

"No. I just flashed on a picture. You know I don't really do people, but it came to me. He's so cute! A redhead. And he's gonna keep his blue eyes."

Tig leaned in to kiss her. "Someday that will be us."

"I know."

"For now, let's practice!"

Sixteen

The next day dawned dreary and gray, as summer days in California beach towns so often do.

The night had not been interrupted by a call from Janie, so as Elizabeth readied for work, she dialed Janie's cell. Mid-ring, she thought perhaps she should have called Terry.

It went to voicemail and she left a message. Animal care done, she and Tig met at the coffee pot.

"Ride today?" she asked.

"Let's take separate cars. We're burning down a house in Rocky Beach today and I don't know how long it will take. We have a review class first and then we burn!" He grabbed her in a tight hug and gave her a smacking kiss.

"Whew! I know you fire guys like to burn stuff, but take it easy," she teased. "See you tonight then."

Tig left first. Elizabeth moved more slowly, checking on Edward's progress. His ears looked a little less curled and she wondered if they would look normal when healed. His appetite continued to improve. Teddy had shown him the cat door in the living room. She sent both Teddy and Edward pictures of hawks and owls circling overhead as a warning. Teddy was much too big to be taken by flying predators, but Edward was still snack-sized.

I know, Mom. I'll take care of him.

Don't go far from the cat door. He is not faster than something that flies.

I know. Teddy was impatient.

Elizabeth gave them each a kiss and headed to work. The drive was gloomy and the weather gray even in town, which was unusual.

Pulling into the Division lot she saw the bustle of the class Tig had mentioned. The recruits gathered around piles of equipment and gear and several senior fire fighters held forth. She felt the buzz of excitement as she crossed to the main building. She saw Tig and noticed again how nicely his uniform fit. Especially from the back.

Denny was already there pulling files from a box.

"Morning. Ready for this?"

"No. It went so well yesterday, I can't wait to get at it," Elizabeth said sourly.

"Somebody needs coffee." Denny rose to pour her a cup.

"Sorry. It was just hard on my one brain cell yesterday. I'm going to get it right today."

"It took me a week to figure it out. You're doing great."

"Who trained you? I have a great trainer."

"I had to figure it out myself with the manual and six thousand calls to technical support."

"See, you are a genius. Thanks," Elizabeth accepted the fresh coffee.

"Okay," Denny started to give instructions.

Elizabeth interrupted. "Let me see if I can at

117

least open it myself."

Denny sat on the edge of the desk and watched as Elizabeth opened the data base and entered her password. She pulled a report to her and clicked open a new window. Carefully she entered the date and report number, slowly moving the mouse from window to window instead of hitting the ENTER button as she'd done so often yesterday. At the end, she hit ENTER and was thrilled to note all the information was in the correct place.

"Yeah!" Elizabeth and Denny high-fived. "Oh, my God, I'm a sweatball!" Elizabeth said. "You'd think I was performing surgery or something. And that only took me," she checked the clock, "eleven minutes. Crap. At this rate, I'll be ninety before I do a year's worth."

"Don't worry. We're a small county."

"Thanks a lot. Okay, anything I can do to speed this up?"

"No. You did it perfectly. Practice will make it go faster. I tried to train Joey and it was like working with a spider monkey. Just as smelly and not as smart."

Elizabeth let out a hoot of laughter.

"That's why we had to hire somebody. Well, you."

Joey threw open the door and it crashed against the coffee maker table.

"Hey, we were just talking about you," Denny greeted him.

"Fuck," he replied.

"Hi, Joey," Elizabeth said. "What's wrong?"

Joey slammed into the office chair at the opposite desk. The chair rolled back and his feet flew up a couple inches, his mouth a large O of surprise.

Face red, he said, "Nothing," and what sounded like 'bitch' mumbled under his breath.

Elizabeth looked at Denny and shrugged.

"Party's over," Denny said.

The morning passed quickly with Denny and Elizabeth working on reports. The contents of the box dwindled appreciably but the atmosphere was marred by Joey's surly presence lurking at the corner desk. He answered phones, but only because Captain Hutchins had come in and admonished him, which both women pretended to ignore.

Elizabeth was so intent on which windows took what data she forgot to pay attention to the data itself until one report stopped her. It read exactly like the fire Tig had described to her. A warehouse in the same area, the roof falling in. Not Tig's fire, but something about it read the same. The tone of the report, while not specifying fault, suggested the building had been unsafe and was empty of life, and the men were ordered in anyway. The roof had fallen and a fire fighter was slightly injured. A follow-up note said the fire fighter, Brian Espinoza, recovered fully.

Hmmm. Brian Espinoza. He was Terry's partner, wasn't he? Elizabeth checked the Captain. Jensen. She had met him on her paper run to the Bay Station.

"Hey, Denny. Isn't Captain Jensen at the Bay Station?" Brian wasn't from the Bay station, so

119

what's with that?

"Nope. He's a swing Captain."

Elizabeth knew a swing Captain 'swung' into any station whose Captain was sick, on vacation, or absent for whatever reason. The good ones got stations pretty quickly, but the not so good ones could stay swing captains forever.

The date on the report was three years old. Long time for a swing captain. Jensen had seemed capable, intelligent, and helpful when she'd gone to get the paperwork. It's nothing. Just tired. Her cell rang and she checked the ID. Janie!

"Taking a break," she called and ran out of the office. "Hey, Janie! How are you! How's the baby?"

"Good! We're both fine. Terry's fine, too. I finally got him to go home and rest.

"What's his name?"

"So you know it's a boy, huh? I'm not gonna ask. Garrett. Garrett Jackson Peterson. How's that?"

Elizabeth was stunned. They'd given their son Tig's birth name as his middle name.

"I don't know what to say. Does Tig know?"

"I don't think so. We kept it a surprise."

"What if it was a girl?"

"Jackie!"

Elizabeth felt herself tearing up. "Oh, Janie. Can I see him today? And you?"

"Sure. Come after work. They're going to boot me out tomorrow. You know these drive through hospitals nowadays. I'll give you all the juicy details."

"I'm so happy for you. Hey, is all that Winnie the Pooh stuff in your nursery just a coincidence?" Elizabeth referred to her husband's childhood nickname. When Tig was a boy, he loved Tigger from Winnie the Pooh. He went around 'being' Tigger and the nickname stuck. Most people thought it was short for Tiger, which was much more manly and acceptable at the fire department. Only Elizabeth, their families and a few close friends knew the truth.

"Sort of. I love Winnie the Pooh, too. Terry was always a Mickey Mouse fan, so maybe for baby number two, we'll switch! We can give you the Winnie nursery ensemble."

"Aren't you getting ahead of yourself a little? How's nursing?"

"Ouch. Speaking of, they're bringing me my little vampire now. For a creature with no teeth, he's got a helluva bite. Gotta go."

"See you later. Sixish, kay?"

Elizabeth texted Tig and asked if he wanted to visit Janie with her. Maybe get some dinner in town. She knew he wouldn't reply quickly, since he was in Rocky Beach burning down a house. She smiled thinking of Tig's excitement. Firemen loved fires.

Back in the office, Denny was sailing out to lunch, meeting her boyfriend. Elizabeth decided to keep working and perhaps improve her speed.

She continued but felt increasingly distracted and her mind wandered to the issue of the mis-filed, or mis-used data base. She gave into curiosity and

121

used her new knowledge to pull up reports filed by Tig. She saw the newer ones could be cross-referenced by name of person filing, by captain in charge, type of incident, or by date. What they didn't say was who input the data. Not a big deal, but if her conspiracy theory held water--she laughed at her spy leanings--someone could input incorrect data and it couldn't be traced. Currently, her password indicated she was using the data base, but it wouldn't account for specific reports input. And, continuing her spy world theory, someone could easily use another password to access the data base.

She held her head in her hands. One thing at a time. Sheesh. Soon she'd have the Russians involved.

Okay, back to Tig's reports. The most recent was the warehouse fire a few days ago. She perused the written report and then clicked on the photos. Stunned, she quickly went from picture to picture and then started over. This fire was almost identical, even down to the building, to the warehouse fire several years ago. The physical photos in the file could almost be copies of those in the data base. She shivered. Probably nothing. A fire is a fire is a fire and a warehouse was probably pretty much like any other warehouse. Right?

Uncomfortable now, she glanced at Joey. He was staring right at her.

"Aren't you going to go to lunch?" he asked. Seemed like he emphasized the word 'go'.

"I'm just going to catch up here. I am really slow at this." Joey squinted at her. He probably thought it made him look speculative and knowledgeable, but it really made him look myopic.

"Well, I'm going then. Get the phones." He left the office without waiting for her answer.

"Sure. Love to." She hadn't realized what a presence he had until he was gone. She physically shook herself and refocused on the computer.

"Terry's fire," she mumbled as she put in his name. It wouldn't come up, so perhaps he didn't file the report. Of course he didn't, duh, he'd been hurt.

Who was at the hospital that day? Who was his captain? That's right, Macbeth. She entered his name and came up with lots of reports. She needed her pocket calendar to find the date and bring up that report. It read straightforward. Except for the dugout hole in the floor. Homemade basement or fire fighter trap? Nothing else caught her eye. She clicked on the photos and again, caught her breath. This was Edward's house. Edward had been living under this house until the fire. Edward had seen someone, a man he said, start this fire. A shiver ran up her spine. Things were coming together, but in what way? And what did it all mean?

Arson was always bad, but this seemed to target fire fighters. Why?

She didn't know how long she had until someone came into the office. She felt like a criminal as she printed out the two fire reports: Tig's warehouse fire and Terry's house fire. She pulled the hard copy of the other warehouse fire and put that in her bag also, instead of in the to-be-shredded box.

She felt an urgency now, to find relevant

information and save it before it was destroyed, mis-filed or mis-entered. It seemed the accidents were more frequent than before. What happened that made this person or persons up the ante?

The phone rang, startling her. "Hello? I mean Division, how can I help you?"

A request for a document pick up from Cove Station, one town north along the coast.

"I can be there in half an hour." She hung up and shut down her computer. She could make it there and back to town in time to meet Janie at the hospital. And maybe Tig for dinner.

Her stomach growled and she decided to stop at Taco Temple, her favorite stop in the little town of Cove.

Seventeen

Leaving Division was relatively easy traffic-wise, and Elizabeth was soon on the highway headed north to the coast. Ten miles of farmland, the prison and the Sheriff's Department, and she was steps from the beach as highway met ocean at the little town of Cove. She bypassed the town a couple miles to Taco Temple. She ordered her taco to go to.

She could have eaten two but didn't want to spoil her appetite for Tig. *Well*, she thought, *that didn't come out right, however accurate it might be.*

Napkin in her lap, she drove and ate. She took the frontage road back to the newly completed fire station. For years after a particularly nasty earthquake had damaged the old building, the fire service had been housed in what amounted to a large circus tent. It embarrassed her to think that was how the citizens of Cove valued their fire fighters, but perhaps she didn't have all the facts. What mattered was that now they were housed in a large, comfortable station.

She had never been to this new station, so she parked on the street in front of a pedestrian door. The service doors were closed and she didn't want to walk around the building knocking or calling. From Tig's stories, she had gathered that people off the street were not always welcome in the domain of the

125

fire station.

She opened the door and called, "Hey, it's Elizabeth from Division. Come to collect some records."

A shuffling noise and a young man opened an inner door. "Yes, can I help you?" His uniform was clean but rumpled, and a slight crease down his face suggested he might have been caught napping. Tig told her that naps were coveted during down time. She controlled a smile.

"Hi. I'm from Division. I came to pick up records from you guys."

"Oh. Okay. Lemme check." He clearly wasn't informed about this. He shuffled away and Elizabeth hoped he wouldn't doze off again on his search for help.

She sat in the lone chair in the anteroom but didn't have a long wait. The man returned bearing a box.

"Sorry about that. This is all the Cap found right now. He says we'll let you know if there's more."

On a hunch, Elizabeth asked, "Cap who?"

"Jensen. He wasn't sure where the other stuff is, if there is more."

"Oh. Swing, huh?"

His face showed surprise, either at her use of the terminology or her knowledge of Jensen. It was some small satisfaction that he now looked more awake.

"Here you go." He handed her the box. She was slightly miffed that he didn't offer to carry it to

126

her car. At Division they had offered to help right away. Well, not really. She had bribed them with cookies.

She trundled her box to the car, doubly glad that she had parked on their doorstep instead of in the lot. A glance at her cell phone showed no return texts, but also the time. Running late.

She hopped back on the highway and sped, only a little over the limit, back to town. The hospital was near the highway so she was able to swing into the parking lot in good time. Finding an empty space was another matter and she finally parked on a side street, not in the lot or the brand new parking structure.

"Crap!" Elizabeth had forgotten to get a toy, or flowers, or even a card for Janie. Some friend. She stopped in the hospital gift shop and quickly chose a card with a baby on the front. She scribbled her and Tig's names inside and grabbed the elevator to maternity. In the hall she checked again for messages from Tig. Nothing. Must be a good fire. Sometimes the guys went out for a beer after a long day, but usually he'd let her know. He did lose track of time easily, though. She excused him.

She entered Janie's room gently, in case she was sleeping. She wasn't, but the little bundle on her chest was.

"Hi," Janie said.

Elizabeth bent to kiss her. "Hi. How are you?" she whispered.

"Doing pretty good. You don't have to whisper. I want him to get used to his noisy little world." She stroked the nearly bald head, a few soft, coppery hairs sticking up.

"Oh, my God. He's so cute. Guess what? I knew he was a boy!" Elizabeth blurted, unable to help herself.

"What? When? All along?"

"No, just since the day you came back from the hospital after Terry's accident. It just popped in."

"And you didn't tell me?"

"You said you didn't want to know."

"I guess not." Janie bent to kiss her son. "I love this little pulse here," she indicated the top of his head. "We call it his 'alien spot.' It's so soft." She sighed.

"Oh, here." Elizabeth handed her the envelope with 'Garrett' written on it.

Janie opened it and laughed, which did wake the baby. He merely blinked sleepily.

"What's so funny?"

"Congratulations on your graduation," Janie read. "Love, Elizabeth and Tig."

"Oh. I'm sorry. I forgot to get you anything so I stopped in the gift shop downstairs, and uh," she studied the front of the card. "I guess that baby's wearing a graduation cap, huh? I didn't really see it. When I opened it to sign, all I saw was Congratulations."

Janie wore a huge grin. "So, Little One, this is your Auntie Elizabeth. The silly one."

Elizabeth felt the blush warm her face. "I'll take it back and get something else." She held out her hand.

128

Janie pulled the card away. "Not on your life. This goes in his scrap book. For evidence." She tucked the card under her.

"Now that he's awake, want to hold him?"

"Absolutely." They completed the baby pass and Elizabeth sat cradling him. "He smells so sweet. Is he always this mellow?" She watched the baby watching her, little fists under his chin, his jaw working at imaginary nursing.

"So far, but he's a redhead, so I doubt he'll stay mellow for long. Terry's got a temper, but I'm sweet as pie, so it'll even out."

They laughed because although Janie didn't have a quick temper, she was very excitable.

"Oh, I've got to go." Elizabeth reluctantly handed over Garrett. "He's just darling. I'll babysit any time. Unless he's sick. Or teething. Or a terrible two. Or a teenager."

"Thanks a lot." Janie smiled. Even post-delivery and with probably not much sleep, she looked lovely.

Elizabeth gave her a good-bye kiss. "Remember if you need a ride home tomorrow, you call me and I'll be there."

"You have a real job now. You can't just run off all the time."

"I know. I keep forgetting that! But I'll come up with something if you need me."

Elizabeth checked her cell phone again while she waited for the elevator. Nothing.

On the main floor she decided to cut through Emergency to the residential street she'd parked on.

129

She entered from the hospital side and saw several ambulances and fire trucks at the entrance.

She was going to scoot around the chaos when she saw Captain Macbeth, still in bunker gear, face blackened with soot. She made her way to him.

"I'm glad you made it. That was fast. Are you okay?" he asked her.

"What?" Elizabeth was caught off-guard.

"I'm sure he'll be fine. He wasn't in there long."

"What?" Elizabeth's heart sped up and adrenaline spurted so fast she was woozy. "Tig," she said faintly.

Macbeth saw her distress and grabbed her shoulders, pulling her into the Emergency waiting room. He sat her on the vinyl chair and said, "Tig. Training fire. He was hurt. He'll be okay." Even in her dazed state Elizabeth knew he had gone from 'I'm sure he'll be fine,' to 'he'll be okay.' Her face must have looked awful, God knows she felt awful, because he suddenly shoved her head over her knees, said, "Breathe," and called for air. Her face was raised and a mask placed over her mouth and nose. Immediately she felt more clear-headed.

"Tell me."

"I don't know. I wasn't in there with him." She eyed his attire and smelled the smoke on him. "I was in another area. Not with Tig." She stared at him. "I'll get someone. Wait here."

Like she would go anywhere even if she could. She watched the bustle around her. She realized she didn't even know where they had taken him. Her heart contracted at the thought of losing him. Not to a training exercise. Not even in a fire. Her mind refused to grasp it. He was so careful. That's why he was called in to train others. His skills and expertise. He couldn't be hurt. Well, he *was* hurt. But not badly, right? Right.

A young woman, face sooty, in a navy blue tee, bunker pants and boots sat down beside her. "I'm Miranda. You're Elizabeth, right?" Elizabeth could only nod and breathe.

"Tig Murphy is your husband?" Another nod.

"Captain Macbeth said to tell you what happened. I'll do that as best I can. We were doing a controlled burn on a donated house and we were given a set of circumstances for rescue and such." She paused to make sure Elizabeth was keeping up. "The training staff had gone through the house first before we lit it up but none of us had." Elizabeth surmised Miranda was a trainee.

"Why are you telling me this, and not an incident commander?"

"I'm not sure." Miranda looked uncomfortable. "I'm not even sure I'm supposed to talk about it, but Captain Macbeth said you were a wife and to fill you in. I'm one of the few who wasn't injured."

Elizabeth let that sink in a moment. "Macbeth?"

"I think he's okay, but he's got a lot of explaining to do. I also think he didn't want to give you the bad news. He usually gets someone else to do that, from what I understand." She smiled and Elizabeth knew she was trying to make her feel better, but she had no patience.

"Go on."

"I only know my part, but I was with Murphy, your husband, when we entered the dwelling. We all had partners and I don't know about everyone else, but they told me so much stuff I knew I wouldn't remember it all. Plus, this was my first fire, first for a lot of us, and even though it was training, it was a real fire, not in the training building, you know?" Elizabeth did know. The training building had safety measures built in, ways to shut off fuel sources, air, known exits, all kinds of devices that a real fire, or a real building site, didn't have.

"I couldn't see. The smoke was so thick, you couldn't even hear. I was really nervous. I knew Murphy was right with me, but I couldn't see or hear. Our job was to search for the kids. Well, pretend kids. And kids like to hide in a fire. They'll go under beds or inside cupboards or closets. There was furniture in this house, too, and we kept tripping and bumping. It doesn't matter what they tell you in a class, it's completely different out there."

Elizabeth flashed on her Doodle rescue. That was outdoors but still the smoke had been instantly oppressive. Ash had floated down in sheets obscuring vision and hearing. She truly couldn't imagine what being inside a house on fire would be like. She feared for Tig every time he was on duty, but didn't allow herself to dwell on it. What good would it do?

"What happened?"

"I was in the lead and we went into a back bedroom. Murphy went to the closet. The floor gave way. I didn't see him because I was looking under the bed. The smoke was so thick." She paused recollecting. "I stood up and didn't see him. I thought maybe he'd gone out the room ahead of me, and I was just going for the door when I heard a voice say, 'Help.' At first I thought it was just somebody fooling around the way they do. They're always testing the recruits, but especially me, because I'm female. They don't think I should be there in the first place. It sucks." She took a deep breath. "Anyway, I stopped, and I heard it again. I still couldn't see, but I worked back to the closet and felt around. He was sticking up out of the floor. When the floor caved, he fell straight in and his air bottle caught him in the opening. His bell bent all to shit and his arm sticking up. I had to get really close to see him. His face mask had been jacked around in the fall. He looked bad. I touched his hand so he'd know I was there and then got help. It took a bunch of us to get him out. We had to lift him straight up. We didn't want to bend anything because of neck or back injuries. Anyway, that's my story. If you have any questions--"

"Mrs. Murphy?" a nurse in scrubs asked from the doorway. "The doctor will see you now."

Elizabeth rose as her heart fell.

Eighteen

"Yes?" Elizabeth took off the oxygen mask and faced the nurse.

"Follow me."

Elizabeth trailed behind the nurse through the Emergency treatment doors to an area with a horseshoe shaped group of desks and work stations surrounded by a larger horseshoe of individual curtained cubicles. Most of the curtains were closed, meaning the cubicles were occupied. The smell of smoke was pervasive and Elizabeth remembered Miranda saying she was one of the few who wasn't injured. Her brain flitted briefly over that, wondering what went wrong in such a controlled practice fire that put so many at risk.

The nurse stopped outside a curtain and turned to her.

"Mrs. Murphy, your husband is fine. He sustained smoke inhalation and some minor injuries. He's got a sore neck and back and he dislocated his shoulder. It's back in place and sore. We've got him on pain meds. The doctor will fill you in on the rest." She spoke so quickly Elizabeth found herself holding her breath so she wouldn't miss anything. She was waiting for the 'but' however, the nurse only yanked the curtain back and let her enter.

Tig's eyes were closed and he looked peaceful. Well, he looked too peaceful, but she scolded herself for her morbid thoughts. She moved to him and took his hand, quickly assessing what she could see. His face was still dirty from smoke except where they had cleaned and bandaged an injured area on the right side. Specks of blood clung to his curly hair. He wore a neck brace. Other squares of white were in startling contrast to his tan arms. More scrapes. She kissed his hand and he opened his eyes.

"Hey, you. How are you?" she asked. She felt tears build and refused to let them fall. It was hard seeing him lie there when she was used to him up and around and wild and funny.

"I feel great." He smiled. It was a little hard to understand him under the oxygen mask. "Good drugs."

She smiled back. "I just bet. They say you're gonna be fine. I think I can take you home after you get a little less, uh, wasted."

"I like wasted." He looked tired but at least he wasn't in pain.

"That was some training, huh?" She clung to his hand. She couldn't stop her heart from beating faster at the thought of the close call.

"Crazy. Floor fell." Something passed over his face she couldn't read. Fear? Pain? Either would be normal.

"Lotsa crazy in our neighborhood lately."

The curtain opened and a tall blond man with a clipboard entered.

"I'm Dr. Jacobsen. Mrs. Murphy?" She

135

nodded. "He's doing fine. He can go home in a while, after we get a few more blood pressure and heart rate readings. You've got paperwork and meds to get so you'll be busy anyway. Can you stay with him today? Or someone?"

"Of course."

"Nothing permanent, here," he perused the chart. "The neck and back need to be watched. You're off work the next three days and before you get returned even to light duty, you need to see your own physician. Then if the back and neck feel okay, a week or so of light duty, another checkup and then you can assume your regular work. I'm sending you home with pain meds. You're going to be the best judge of your pain and activity levels. All your injuries were superficial but that doesn't mean they should be ignored, so give yourself time to heal. Any questions?" He looked at each of them. "No? I'll get your discharge papers ready. Nicetameetcha." He whipped out of the curtain again.

"Wow. That was exhausting." Elizabeth turned to Tig. His eyes had slid shut. She pulled a chair next to his bed and waited for the discharge papers.

With gratitude that he was safe, she reviewed what Miranda had told her. Her only conclusion was that someone was out to hurt fire fighters. Maybe it was time to alert someone higher up. But who? She didn't know what was going on. She needed to talk to Tig, she decided. After he was home and resting.

She must have dozed in her chair because the curtain ripping back startled her. The same nurse blew in with a clipboard and two white pharmacy bags. Elizabeth barely listened to the instructions since she knew everything was written on the discharge sheet. She signed many places and the nurse whipped away again.

Tig was awake and she carefully helped him dress in his soiled uniform. As she gathered up her purse and papers, an orderly arrived with a wheelchair.

"I hate this part," said Tig as he allowed himself to be guided into it.

"I know. But I can't carry you to the car, so enjoy the ride," Elizabeth said.

"Ma'am," the orderly said, "why don't you pull your car up to the Emergency doors, and I'll wait with him."

"Good idea." Elizabeth ran for her car and when she drove up, the orderly had the chair out front. Tig looked small and dazed sitting there and she almost couldn't stop her tears. She busied herself moving the passenger seat back and finding her picnic blanket to tuck around him after the orderly helped Tig into the car. Tig fell asleep almost as soon as the car was in motion and Elizabeth was left to her thoughts on the half hour drive home. She mused that they would have to pick Tig's car up at some point. It was probably still at Division.

She sent pictures to Teddy and when she pulled into the drive and both cats greeted her on the porch. Edward looked so small next to Teddy, but his injuries were nearly healed. His ears would probably always be curly and they made him look like an irreverent elf with his narrow pixie face. *Some Siamese in there*, Elizabeth thought as she unlocked the front door.

She woke Tig and helped him all the way to the bed. *Thank goodness we didn't buy a two-story house.*

What a day. She tucked Tig in and lay next to him. She started to shake and finally let herself cry, trying not to disturb him. She felt both cats jump on the bed. Teddy settled between them by their feet, and Edward lay by her side near the edge of the bed. Tig rolled toward her and felt for her hand.

"'Sokay," he mumbled.

She finally drifted off, still holding Tig's hand, Teddy's gentle snoring a normal accompaniment.

Tig woke in the night and she was up instantly. She dosed him with pain meds and checked for fever. He fell back asleep but she couldn't.

Not wanting to wake him, she went to the kitchen and made a cup of peppermint tea. Teddy followed.

Hi, Mom. You okay?

I guess so. Why aren't you sleeping with Tig?

Just wanted to check on you. As long as I'm up, maybe I'll have a bite.

Elizabeth smiled. Teddy was always willing to have a bite, and that was why he was such a substantial cat. The neighbor's son had once said, after giving Teddy a nice belly rub, 'Teddy's not a big cat, he's a lot of little cats.'

138

She didn't feel like watching TV. She wasn't much of a TV person anyway, except for watching movies with Tig. She was a reader, but had left her book in the bedroom and didn't want to risk waking Tig to get it.

She went to her car and dragged out the box of records from Cove Station. She settled on the couch with a blanket over her, her tea next to her, and Teddy right where she needed the files.

Teddy, can you be more in the way? He just looked inscrutable. *Fine.*

She pulled a stack of folders, leaving the box on the floor. It quickly became evident these files were not stored in any order, but had been thrown into the box at random, perhaps to mollify those at Division, rather than help organize records.

She sorted them into piles and chose the pile most likely to assist her in looking for more evidence of arson or what she termed target fires: a fire fighter hurt or the report reading like the others she'd found.

She found a couple of possibles, but the files thrown into the box were not helpful. Maybe that was the point. Give Division files that don't show anything. It was Captain Jensen who had authorized these files. He was only a swing captain, so maybe it was just the way it worked out? Still, the files could only be less helpful if they'd not been there at all. That was food for thought.

Teddy snored on, conveniently located in the middle of her piles. She smiled and rubbed his belly, causing him to roll, expose more of its vast expanse, purr and smile.

"Good idea, buddy," she said. She finally felt ready to go back to bed. She repacked the files and put the box near the door. She would be taking care of Tig tomorrow, so that box would have to wait to go to Division. It should be no problem, especially since no one wanted the job she had taken. With good reason, she thought. She snuck back into bed with Tig, who didn't move a muscle. He slept on his side, neck brace propped on one of his many pillows.

Just as she got herself arranged a thump on the bed indicated Teddy was back, too.

Night, guys.

Night, Mom, from Teddy. Gentle snores from Tig and Edward.

Nineteen

Tig woke Elizabeth early when he got up to use the bathroom. She saw the pain he was in and guided him back.

"Coffee or tea?" she asked. For both of them, the choice of morning beverage was an indicator of health. Coffee meant well, tea meant someone didn't feel good.

"Tea," he said.

"You got it. Let me get you some toast to take your meds with. Don't take them on an empty stomach," she warned. "I'll get the paper while things are cooking."

She started the tea water, put bread in the toaster, then dashed into the damp, misty morning to get the paper. The plastic bag around it was soaked so she left that on the counter.

"Here you go." She put the paper next to Tig and turned on his bedside light. "Be right back with toast and tea."

"Okay, guys, you're next, just wait," she told Teddy and Edward who had come to expect a dab of canned food as their breakfast service.

She brought back brown rice tea, Tig's cure for anything that ailed him, and sourdough toast, lightly margarined.

"Want help sitting up?" she asked.

He shook his head and painfully scooted upright.

"Take your meds and then eat. You'll feel better soon. They said it was all muscular and not permanent but you should be careful."

Tig grimaced in response and swallowed several pills with slugs of hot tea. He adjusted the heating pad on the small of his back and sighed.

"Thanks."

"You're welcome. Can I get you anything else?"

"No, thanks."

"Okay, I'll just be in the kitchen. I'll take my cell and text me if you want anything, okay? Then you don't have to yell."

Tig's face looked pale and she felt his forehead. Couldn't help it. "No fever. Okay, I'll go now." That got a small smile.

In the kitchen she doled out two small dishes of canned food to the delight of the cats. She brewed a cup of coffee for herself and sat in her meditation chair. It had been a while since she'd done a proper grounding. Things had moved so fast lately.

She let herself put down 'roots' and started a regeneration cycle of energy, dropping negative and cycling in positive. She let go of all the hectic energy and called back that which she had sent out in the last few days. She felt a bit replenished.

She didn't really read people, but some she could. Tig, because it was natural for those she loved. Baby Garrett was a surprise, but she loved

Janie and Terry and sometimes sent feelers of energy to them. It was hard to explain to others. People's energy was often closed down or disguised, but animals were pretty open, especially if she asked permission to 'converse.' They naturally communicated in pictures more often than words, so it was second nature to send out pictures of her own almost subconsciously. She could tune in even when she wasn't trying.

One day as she drove down her street she heard a voice saying, *Let's go, come on! Let's go! Hurry!* and saw a large black dog leaping and circling its owner by a car parked near a popular hiking trailhead. Another time she was driving in the city, and heard, *Do you mind? Just scoot over a little.* And then, *I can't! You see how crowded it is? Where do you think I can go? I'm squished as it is.* She couldn't place that conversation until she looked up as she waited at a red light. The power lines were filled, pole to pole with sparrows, jostling and adjusting for space.

Sometimes her work, her hobby, her gift, whatever people wanted to call it, was so entertaining. It was also rewarding to help an animal who otherwise couldn't communicate. Sometimes it was heartbreaking.

She let her energy go out to Tig. He was in pain but that eased as the meds kicked in. He still had residual fear from the fall and she tried to release some of that. She sent comforting energy and protection over him. Teddy and Edward had finished their breakfasts and had joined Tig on the bed as he

143

read the paper. Attempted to, rather. Teddy lay right next to Tig's thigh, on top of the remaining newspaper sections, while Edward had oozed into his lap under the front page. Tig was reading with difficulty, due to his injuries and too much 'help.'

Elizabeth smiled and slowly let herself come back into her own body. Sometimes she didn't want to. She bent over and touched the floor, re-grounding herself and relieving the dizziness a deep meditation sometimes brought on.

Still too early to call Division to say she wouldn't be there today. Good day to catch up on housework.

Janie was coming home today! She added that to her list of things to do and people to call.

The morning passed pleasantly relaxing with Tig and an old movie. She made sure he ate and took his medication. The sun was trying to come out by noon and after lunch she needed to get out for a while.

She called Janie's cell.

"Are you home?" Elizabeth asked when Janie picked up.

"Just got in. It feels so good. Terrifying, too, though."

"What do you mean?"

"The only people who know anything about babies are all at the hospital. With Terry and me, it's the blind leading the blind."

"I see what you mean." Elizabeth laughed. "I'm going to the store later. Need anything?"

"No, Terry did a great job of stocking up

before I got home."

"How's Terry doing?"

"Good. He's the only one who's gotten any rest lately. He goes back to work tomorrow. Light duty, nights, so at least I'll have him during the day."

"Don't forget I'm right across the street. Available nights, even, for a small surcharge."

"I won't forget. Okay, we're just watching Garrett watching us. I'm not sure what we're going to do next, but I'd better go in case something exciting happens."

"I'll drop by later, okay? Wanna see that little bundle." Elizabeth didn't tell Janie about Tig, and since she didn't ask, that meant Terry hadn't either. Although he'd been off work, the grapevine was potent and Elizabeth was sure he knew and didn't want Janie to worry. At least not right away.

Elizabeth dashed to the store, not wanting to leave Tig for long. Not because he wasn't doing well, but because he was. As soon as he felt better, whether from a slight cold or something more serious, he'd be out doing yard work or something crazy. She had to keep an eye on him this time.

She worried for nothing. After putting the groceries away she peeked in and all three boys were sound asleep. The paper forgotten on the floor, TV tuned to an old movie, Tig was propped looking pretty uncomfortable with his cervical collar.

He woke as she began to close the door.

"How are you doing?"

"Pretty good. The nursing staff is excellent." He indicated the limp forms of the cats. "They haven't left me alone since you got up."

"Hungry? I'm making burgers with everything."

"Sounds good." An excellent sign since Tig was always hungry.

She returned with sizzling burgers with all the trimmings and joined him on the bed. "Another movie?" she asked.

"Sure. I'm in marathon mode."

Full of burgers and medication, he didn't last half the movie, but that was fine with Elizabeth. He was home. He was healing.

Her cell rang. She muted it and ran out of the bedroom.

"Where are you?" Denny asked.

"Oh, my God. I forgot to call. I'm so sorry. I woke up too early to call in and then forgot."

"Well, where are you?"

"You know the training house fire yesterday?"

"Of course. That's all everyone's talking about. What about it?"

"The accidents?"

"Yeah?"

"My husband was injured there. He was training there and. . ."

"Oh, I'm sorry. I didn't know. Who's your husband?"

"Tig Murphy."

"He's a hottie. How's he doing?" Elizabeth was a bit startled at Denny's assessment, true as it was.

"Uh, fine. Well, not fine now, but he will be."

"Yeah, I heard no one was seriously injured, but boy, people are pissed!"

"What's going on?"

"Huge brouhaha. Brass is rolling in and out of here like ocean waves. And just as cold. Everyone's passing the buck about who's responsible. I bet Tig gets reamed too when he gets back. When will that be?"

"I'm not sure. Probably a week. Why would Tig be in trouble?"

"Because so many people got hurt and he was one of the trainers, right?" Denny didn't wait for a response. "The whole thing was a balls-up and somebody's got to pay. It'll probably be a captain, but you know, it all rolls downhill."

"I guess. Anyway, I won't be in for a couple days."

"Okay. See you." Denny clicked off abruptly.

Elizabeth needed to hear what happened from Tig. Especially if he might be held responsible for the mess. He needed to know now, and not be blindsided.

The next time he awoke, she'd ask. Not something she looked forward to.

Twenty

Tig awoke when Elizabeth slid into bed beside him. He had slept most of the day and looked better for it.

"Anything I can get you?" she asked.

"Not right now, thanks."

"You up to talking about what happened?"

He looked at her enquiringly.

"Denny called and Division is looking for a head to put on a pike. I just wanted to warn you. I also want to hear what happened. A recruit named Miranda told me her end; she was with you, right?"

Tig nodded.

"I've had a lot of time to think about it, but before I get on the bandwagon about a great plot, I thought I should have some facts." She took his hand. "I was really worried." She kissed his palm.

"I was a little worried myself in that house, stuck half out of the floor. What plot are you talking about?"

"Our research into the recent and not-so-recent fires. Arson and how fire fighters seemed to get injured more frequently than usual. I mean, I can't remember the last time someone really got hurt, but now lots of 'accidents' and I'm concerned because it's caught up to us. First Terry, now you. If there weren't so many, I'd think it was personal. Even Brian Espinoza, from Terry's station got hurt.   That's seems a lot for our small area, don't you think?"

Tig nodded. "I think you're right. Something is wrong here. We checked that house thoroughly and that floor had been deliberately weakened so someone would fall through. It is worrisome. I hate to think it but, it pretty much eliminates a citizen."

"Why?"

"Because a citizen wouldn't know we were burning that house, and a citizen wouldn't know the training format and how we looked for 'victims' or how we would proceed." His head flopped onto the pillow. "This is terrible."

"I know. I'm sorry. But if I had to pick someone, I vote for Joey."

"He's pretty unlikeable, I agree. Why him?"

"He's so bitter about being pulled from his training. Or having to re-train. Was he at the fire?"

Tig lifted his head. "Yes. He was. He was awfully enthusiastic, but I have to say, he followed instructions. It makes sense as far as arsonists go. They usually like to see the results of their actions. He had a front row seat."

"Maybe he followed directions so nothing would go wrong with his plan to see someone get hurt. Did he know it would be you in the bedrooms?"

"Yes, but not until we were ready to go in. The training team had it all worked out in advance, but we didn't tell the recruits 'til just before."

Something occurred to Elizabeth. "Where

149

did you keep the training plan?"

"In the office."

"But where? In a file or on the computer?"

"The trainers all had copies, but we kept them pretty well under wraps. You know, to make it more spontaneous for the recruits. The whole file was on the computer."

"And who has nothing but time on the computer in the office all day, every day?"

"Shit." His head flopped back on the pillow.

"I'm not saying it's him, but he's an angry man. Isn't he also at the upper end of the age range for getting in? Didn't you say he'd been rejected before and this was his last shot? You're the one he seems to hold responsible for his latest re-training."

"It's not just me. It's a decision that comes down from several sources based on a lot of information."

"Okay, two things. Either he doesn't know that, and since you're the one giving him the bad news, he thinks it's all your fault and wants to make you pay, or he does know, and wants to punish other people for slowing his progress."

"If it's option one, why are other fire fighters getting hurt, if he blames me?"

Elizabeth gave Teddy a scratch while she thought. "Well, it's weak, but if it's Joey, he seems unstable.   Okay, it's been going on for several years, right? So, what if each time he tried to get on the fire department, he blamed a specific person, just like this time he blamed you?"

"I could see how that makes sense." Tig

opened his pill bottle and swallowed one with water. "I'm so tired. I can't think right now."

"I know. It's awful. I don't know what to do next. Should we talk to someone higher up? We don't have any proof, just speculation."

"The arsons didn't leave any traceable evidence pointing to one person. Everyone has gas and other accelerants lying around the garage. No finger prints, foot prints, or anything we can track."

"I know. Oh! I didn't tell you. Speaking of inadmissible evidence, you know Edward's fire? It is also Terry's fire. I tuned into Edward when he was dreaming and you wouldn't believe it. The house he lived under was Terry's house fire. I saw him under it, and then I saw the house when he ran away. It matches the pictures in the case file. He also saw who started it, but not his face. So, definitely arson, which you probably know."

"Great. Can we put Edward on the stand? Or you? You can testify the cat told you, right?"

Elizabeth knew he was testy because of his close call. Besides, she was used to sarcasm from people who didn't know her well. It still stung a little coming from Tig. He saw her face.

"I'm sorry. I guess I'm a little more shaken up than I thought."

"That's okay. Hungry?"

"Maybe a little."

"Be right back." She went to the kitchen followed by two cats who stirred themselves in hopes of a snack or a fallen treat. She made Tig a ham and cheese sandwich and sure enough, two little

151

scraps of ham fell just in front of Edward and Teddy.

Just one each guys. Too much salt is bad for you.

I like salt, said Teddy.

Mmmph, said Edward, still wrestling with his ham.

She handed Tig his sandwich and sat back on the bed.

"Thanks, this is great."

Tig was getting better.

"What do you think we should do next?"

"Not sure. I guess we need more evidence. Unless this guy, Joey, or whoever, makes a mistake, we've got nothing. I'll let everyone know to be extra careful, but we take all the precautions we can. No one could have predicted yesterday."

"That's what he's counting on. Monday if you're well enough, I'll go back to work and start looking for more reports. Oh, I didn't tell you this either. I copied some reports from a few years ago that fit the same pattern. I'm starting my own file."

"Okay. Just be careful. It might not be Joey."

"Yeah, but he's in the office all the time. I'll double check, but his applications and rejections seem to fit the time frame we're talking about."

"Maybe I'll talk to Terry and Brian, too. See if they remember anything," Tig said.

"Well don't ask about Joey directly, that will prejudice them and maybe stop them from mentioning something or someone else."

"You watch way too many crime shows." Tig pushed himself higher on his pillows.

"I like crime shows. Also, don't tell Terry or Brian *why* you're asking."

"You don't think one of them had anything to do with it? That's crazy."

"You can't be too careful. Besides, they might mention it to someone else and there goes our attempt to keep it quiet and trap him," Elizabeth added.

"Trap him! I don't think so. We're not trapping anybody. We're looking for information to hand over to the brass. That's all."

"Fine." Elizabeth started to say more, but got a good look at Tig in the dim light. He was still pale and the cervical collar made him look vulnerable. She softened.

"Really. Fine. I'll be careful. Want to watch something, or are you ready for sleep?"

"I feel like I could sleep for a long time. I hate this."

"I know. I'm just glad you're okay." She turned out the light and cuddled close, being careful of his arm and neck. Two thumps onto the bed indicated the family was all there.

On Wednesday Tig was vastly improved, and Thursday passed with nothing more exciting than tea in the back yard and watching sports on TV. Elizabeth caught up on chores. She was so busy with Tig she didn't have time to check on Janie or even ask how Terry's first shift back went.

Friday morning roared in too soon and she found herself back on the long road to Division. She left Tig with lots of supplies and admonishment to be careful.

The Division lot was packed and she parked down by the ratty picnic bench. Grumbling, she carted her Cove station box all the way up the slope to the back door of the classroom wing.

Classes were in session and the hall was quiet. Muted voices raised and lowered as she passed each closed door.

Just past the bathrooms she heard a louder voice. A discussion on computers was going on in the last class. It didn't sound fire related, more a technical conversation about websites and access codes, hacking and passwords.

"I could use a class like that," Elizabeth mumbled, out of breath as she reached the outer door.

She staggered up to the main office and dropped the box next to her desk. Denny was already there, as usual.

"Coffee?" she asked.

"Not yet. Water." Elizabeth dug a bottle out of her desk and slugged half of it down. "It's actually warm in town today."

"Gonna get even hotter. This is the only building with A/C so lots of crabby people here today."

"What's going on? The lot's full. I had to park in the boonies."

"Lots of scrambled eggs here today," Denny referred to the golden swirls on the administrators uniforms, "placing blame and pointing fingers."

"Great."

"How's your honey? Nursing him back to health?" Denny waggled her eyebrows.

"He's much better. Otherwise I wouldn't be here today. I think he's going to wrangle a check-up soon, so he can come back to work."

Joey came in, not slamming the door. "Hey."

Elizabeth and Denny exchanged a look. "Hey," they both said.

Elizabeth booted up her computer. "What's going on, Joey? Some fire, huh?"

"Yeah. I was there."

"I heard. What are you doing here? I thought you were back in training."

"I am." He gave her a 'don't push it' look. "I was at the training fire and I'm giving them my report."

"You are, huh?" Denny asked. "I heard everyone has to give their version of events. Not just you."

Joey's face darkened and his relatively sunny mood evaporated. He didn't answer but went to his desk and pulled out some papers, slammed the drawer shut and stalked out of the office.

"Whew," said Elizabeth. "You should be careful. I think he's unstable."

"What? Joey? No, he's just immature. Got a temper, though."

"Don't push his buttons."

"I shouldn't but sometimes I just can't help it. He's such a dick." Denny smiled.

"Yeah, he is that." Elizabeth pulled some files and began to input reports, mentally cataloging what she wanted to copy the minute Denny was out of the office.

She hadn't got far when the door burst open, and several Chiefs she didn't know and several Captains she did, including Jensen, Macbeth and Hutchins, entered all talking at once.

They filed into the inner office. Elizabeth briefly wondered where they would all sit. Immediately the door opened again and Macbeth came out, winked at her and grabbed two office chairs, then whisked the door closed. His was the voice she'd heard in the classroom. The computer discussion.

"Hey, Denny. Do they train the recruits on computers?"

"Sure. Why?"

"I overheard a little of the class and it seemed really interesting. Maybe I could sit in and learn something. I don't know much about computers, except email and web surfing. This sounded really cool about hacking and passwords and things."

Denny shook her head. "That's not a recruit class. They just get the basics. What did you hear?"

"I think it was Macbeth talking. Sounded cool."

"Oh, that's it. Macbeth used to do computer work for some corporation in town before he joined up. I think he moonlights fixing computers and things. You know fire fighters, everyone's got a second job. Anyway, it paid great but he wanted to do something meaningful, or so I heard."

Elizabeth went back to entering files, trying

not to make mistakes out of sheer boredom. A couple of times she caught herself hitting ENTER at the wrong place. In frustration she stopped and took a break.

She called Tig. All was well at the homestead, although he was restless. He'd made a doctor's appointment for that afternoon.

"Don't drive if you've had your pain meds," Elizabeth said.

"Nope, I've been good. Ask the cats. Just Ibuprofen. Wanted to test my limits. I'm in danger of going stir crazy. Took the collar off and I finally feel like I'm not being strangled."

"Okay, then."

"Really. I'm good. Ready to ride a desk for a while. My brain is decomposing from disuse."

Elizabeth laughed. "Okay. Text me what the doc says."

"Will do. How's it going there?"

"It's a zoo. All the admin in a fluster. Haven't overheard anything though. I'm still looking for files."

"Be careful. Gotta get ready for my appointment. Love you."

"Love you, too."

She turned to re-enter the office and saw Captain Jensen watching her. She flushed. Had he heard her comment about looking for files?

"Hi, Captain. How's it going in there?" she asked nervously.

"Hard to say." He seemed speculative. Elizabeth thought she was being paranoid and scuttled back to the office. She noted Jensen watched her retreat. She shook it off and returned to the terminal.

The bosses' meeting must have finished. The inner office door was open and she didn't hear any discussion. Just to be safe, she peeked inside. Empty. Denny was also out, so she copied the suspicious files, breathing a sigh when they were back in the stack and her copies stashed in her tote. She wondered briefly if it was some sort of crime to have copies. *It's not like it's a police report*, she reasoned. *Still, probably at least a little illegal.* She smiled to herself as she thought of another Tig-and-Elizabeth line, 'it's only wrong if you get caught.' She did watch a lot of crime shows.

She continued her file load, finding a few more she wanted to copy. By three o'clock she still hadn't heard from Tig. She ate a granola bar at her desk and decided to do another hour and leave early, since she hadn't taken a lunch break. The office remained quiet and she found that a little disturbing. Denny hadn't returned and neither had Joey. The admin was also absent. She heard the muted bustle of the station part of Division, the living quarters and work of the men and women on duty. The classrooms were far enough away and the office windows faced so she couldn't see the training activity. It was creepy, wondering what was going on with the higher ups that might affect Tig. And her.

Numbers swam before her and she made more mistakes. She decided to try out her, or Tig's theory, and opened a search screen and put in a random date in the report number window, just to see what happened. Nothing exciting. She got a report, but it was actually a supply requisition.

She put in another date. This time she got a real report, a medical call. At least the theory had merit: if you put information in the wrong window, you did get something.

Not sure how this was helpful, she put in the date of Terry's fire and hit a bulls eye. The report was there. No one would find it unless they had a report number. You would have to search by date in the report number window, and that meant whoever put the data in could cover himself, or herself, she amended, if it was discovered. *Who would want to bury the reports and why? I mean, wouldn't it be better not to have it at all if you wanted to hide something?*

She sighed. Another mystery. At least she knew things could conveniently be lost. The computer equivalent to misfiling a folder. No one could say for sure if it was intentional. Why would Joey do that? To hide arson reports or injury reports from a data base search? She tried that. She put in 'injuries on duty' and got nothing. She tried a few more permutations but the search engine was not designed for that. It simply read data, and if you didn't have the correct numbers to look for, you got no useful information.

Marginally inspired, she looked for personnel files to check Joey's applications versus his rejections. She could not enter the secure part of the data base. Figures.

159

She eyed the open door of the inner office. Lots of file cabinets in there. Maybe personnel records? Although lots of things were done online now, an applicant would still have to supply school transcripts, letters of reference, something tangible for a paper trail. All quiet here. Toward the end of the work day, Division slowed down, more like a working fire station now as non-fire employees left for the day.

She entered the inner office and saw several metal four-drawer file cabinets along the far wall. She closed the blinds that allowed the Captain to see the engine bay and hoped that didn't look suspicious to anyone. Oh, well. All the cabinets were locked.

"Crap." Of course they would be. Her heart beat faster every minute she was in there. She had no business in that office. Nothing she could say would get her out of trouble if she was caught. She moved faster. Quickly she pulled open desk drawers looking for keys to the file cabinets. Security was not that great. She found a set of small keys in the paperclip box. Not a bad place since the keys blended in with all the metal.

Sweaty hands plied the keys in the locks and one at a time she opened the drawers. They screeched. There was no mistaking the sound of a three foot metal drawer opening. She rifled files quickly. No personnel folders. Each drawer seemed louder than the last until she thought her heart would explode. Nothing. She closed the drawers, made sure they were locked and returned the keys to the desk. The phone rang in the outer office.

160

"That was a waste and I just about had a heart attack." She grabbed the receiver noting the phones had been quiet all afternoon. "Division, this is Elizabeth."

"Hi, Elizabeth, Connie Du Champ from Human Resources. I'm glad I caught you. Need you to get your finger prints done at the county. I'm going to call over and set it up, and you make the appointment at your convenience. Need it by next week though, okay?"

Human Resources! Of course. If she'd thought it through for five minutes, she'd have remembered that all the hiring went through HR. Heart attack for nothing. That left hacking into the computer somehow, since she'd never get into the paper files. *Listen to yourself, hacking into secure files.* As if she could do that. *I'm turning into a first class criminal.*

"Elizabeth?" Connie asked. "Did you get that?"

"Oh, uh, sure. Why do they need my prints?"

"We print all city and county employees. It's been a little crazy lately and I didn't get that information to you. We were so happy we had even one applicant for your job. I guess I shouldn't tell you that."

"No, it's fine. I knew what I was getting into. So, that means all the fire fighters are printed too?"

A moment of silence told Elizabeth her question was odd. "Yes. You're the wife of a fire fighter aren't you? Don't you know that?"

"I probably just forgot."

"Is it a problem?" Connie's voice was decidedly chilly now.

"Oh, no, not at all. I'll call right now."

Connie laughed, the chill gone. "No, call Monday. I have to set it up or they'll charge you."

"Charge me?" Elizabeth's heart sped right up again.

"It's fifty dollars for a non-city or county employee to get printed.

"Oh." Elizabeth sighed. "It costs." It was time to go home. Imagining a criminal charge when the poor lady was trying to save her fifty bucks. Sheesh.

"Sure, I'll call first thing Monday."

"Since it's for us, you can go during work. Don't make it on your lunch hour unless you have to."

"Of course. Thank you."

Elizabeth shut down her computer and shakily gathered her stolen files. *I shouldn't keep these here.* She would start a home collection. *Paranoia, your name is Elizabeth.*

The campus was very quiet when she walked back to her car. The lot had emptied and the overflow where she had parked thinned. She drove out and realized she was still upset. A good excuse not to cook. Take out. That was the solution. She would text Tig to see if Thai was okay. She pulled over, opened her phone and saw that Tig had texted her. Probably during her burglary attempt.

'Doc cleared me for light duty. Going back Monday for half day in the classroom. Yippee!'

'So glad. M bringing Thai for dinner, k? Wat do u want?'

Texting had distinct advantages although it had taken her a while to use abbreviations and deliberate misspellings in any kind of writing. It went against her grain as the daughter of an English major.

She was pretty sure Tig would want his usual, so if she didn't hear back in a few minutes, she'd call their favorite Thai place, Lotus, and hope for the best. She turned up the volume on her phone. At work she kept it on vibrate so if it was noisy (or if she was committing a crime), she couldn't hear it.

A doorbell ring signified Tig's response. She pulled over and checked. Sure enough, green curry chicken, mild. She called Lotus and ordered. It would be ready for pick up by the time she waded through the quitting time traffic and made it back to the 'country.'

She was almost to Lotus' parking lot when she felt alarm or excitement, she couldn't tell which, pouring into her. It wasn't from anything she or the traffic was doing. For safety, she parked near Lotus and sent out her feelers. First she checked Tig. He was resting. Then she checked Teddy. He was very excited. She felt for Edward and he was also excited, and a little alarmed.

What's going on? Hey, you guys, focus. Tell me!

We got a present! Teddy. *A toy! But we're giving it to you!*

Edward? What's going on?
It's really big! Has big teeth!

Elizabeth was worried. Go home or get the food?

Teddy! Tell me. Send me a picture.

An image of a terrified mouse skittered across her mind, like the mouse was skittering across the living room floor. Poor thing had probably come in the pet door. A huge mistake.

She tried to connect with it, but it was frightened and wild. Non-domestic animals were sometimes harder to connect with since they didn't have regular contact with people. She sent it calming energy and told it to hide under something. She would help it when she got home.

She ran in and grabbed the order, rushing the usual small talk with Don and his lovely Thai wife, Lili, who did all the cooking.

Minutes later she unlocked the front door. She put the bags on the dining room table and looked around. No one and nothing in the living room or kitchen. She heard Tig in the bedroom and hurried down the hall.

Tig was just swinging his legs out of bed. Both cats hunched expectantly in front of the dresser.

"Cats chased a mouse in here. It's under the dresser," Tig said.

"I know. I got the advance announcement. I hate their presents. Teddy's getting old,"

"Hey!" Teddy interrupted her,

"Now that he has a young partner in crime, we might be in for more."

Tig grabbed a pair of gloves while Elizabeth quickly emptied the bedside trash can.

"Here," she said, "put it in here."

Tig pulled out the bottom drawer of the dresser and felt around for the mouse. Elizabeth tried to send calming energy to the mouse, but doubted it was in any position to receive it. Two hyper-aroused cats, one giant hand fishing around, and two smelly humans all bent on catching it.

A squeak heralded its capture. Tig set it in the waste can and Elizabeth covered it with a kerchief.

"I'll take it outside, far away." She trotted to the outback and set the can on its side. A large deer mouse, much larger than a regular mouse, emerged undamaged from its experience with the cats. It stared up at her with beautiful dark eyes and an incredibly pointed nose. Gratitude waved toward her and the mouse shot into the brush faster than she thought possible.

In the house she washed her hands. Tig had set the meal on the table.

That was fun! said Edward.

Yes, let's do it again, said Teddy.

Let's not, said Elizabeth.

You don't appreciate our gifts, said Teddy.

I think you're right, said Elizabeth.

Teddy flopped on his back. *That was good.*

Edward climbed into Tig's lap which was fast becoming his place of choice.

"How are you feeling?" she asked Tig.

"That was a very exciting way to wake up," he said. He opened his curry and poured it over the rice in his giant bowl.

"I can imagine." They enjoyed dinner in

companionable silence. The day had been busy for both of them.

Later as they readied for bed, Elizabeth caught him up on her searches. He listened and nodded about her computer data search, but his face turned stony at her rifling the files.

"You could be fired for that. Or I could be."

"No, you're not responsible for what I do."

"I don't know. The way things are going lately, I'm not counting on anything. I have to make a full report about the training fire and then get grilled by the brass Monday. Not looking forward to it. That's almost worth not going back to work for."

"There's something else."

"What?"

"I need you to figure out how to access personnel files."

"You've got to be kidding! I can't do that. There's no way I can explain that if I'm caught!"

"If it's on computer, you won't get caught. It's remote, right?"

"All the crime shows you watch. Don't you know they can trace a computer footprint? They could find out it was me, and that I have no reason to look. That's not in my job description. I'd be history. That's all confidential."

"All right, all right. Keep your hair on. I'll figure out another way."

"Oh, for Pete's sake Elizabeth. You're going to get us both busted. Just let it go."

She didn't say any more, which they both knew was not agreement on her part, but it staved off further argument for now.

They brushed their teeth in somewhat frosty silence and got into bed.

They kissed goodnight and equilibrium was restored. At least for now. Elizabeth wasn't going to give up. Someone had tried to hurt her husband, and that was not acceptable. She would dig until she had something solid to report. She would try not to get arrested or embarrass Tig. He had great promise in the department. If she didn't screw it up for him.

The weekend was spent catching up on chores and more rest for Tig. Elizabeth watched him every time he got up or stepped outside. She could tell he was irritated, but she couldn't help herself.

By Sunday night, they were both glad they would return to work the next day.

Twenty-One

Monday was gray and dreary again at the coast. Elizabeth was heartily sick of the weather, and grateful that Division was in town where it was usually sunny. She and Tig took separate cars since he was on half-day.

They caravanned to Division and parked side by side. A quick kiss and they parted ways.

In the main office, Denny was already at a terminal. She said hi, but didn't look up and the captain's door was shut, both not good signs.

Elizabeth opened her terminal and began to input data. In a couple hours, she was caught up and wondered what to do next. Denny hadn't said two words to her and the Captain's door remained closed. The passage on the engine bay was constantly in use, with somber-looking fire fighters and men in suits walking back and forth.

"Seems like the inquisition," Elizabeth mumbled and was surprised to hear Denny reply.

"Yeah, it's bleak around here. The scuttlebutt is they can't find someone to pin it on, so they're really getting ugly and lots of folks are getting written up. It's a mess."

"Everyone's got to shoulder a piece of the blame whether they deserve it or not, huh?"

"Something like that. Good people are caught in the shit storm and it's not fair. Your hubby won't come out unscathed, I can tell you. He got hurt pretty badly, so maybe they'll go easy, but I don't know."

"I heard lots of people got hurt."

"Yeah, but Tig was among the worst. Most people just had smoke inhalation or minor scrapes."

"How is that possible? I mean, you guys check all the equipment before you go out, right?"

"Supposed to. I imagine they did for a training, to set a good example, but you know, the guys don't always do what they're supposed to. 'If it worked yesterday, it'll work today' sometimes is the older guys' attitude. Maybe this time it caught up to them."

"Multiple equipment failures? Doesn't that sound suspicious to you?"

"I don't know anything. Just telling you what I heard." Denny shut down immediately, returning to her typing.

"Hey, Denny. I'm out of files here. Cove station didn't really give me much. Jensen was the swing Captain out there. I think he just threw some old files in a box. Should I go back? Or call and try to talk to the regular Captain?"

"I'd better call." Denny phoned and arranged for more files. "Okay, tomorrow they'll have more. Talked to a senior man who knows what's what. Jensen's gonna be there a while and he has his head up—never mind. He doesn't know what's going on. Talk to Mike Anselmo tomorrow. He's a sweetheart. Good-looking and always out for the ladies, so you'd better watch out."

"I guess he wasn't there when I went before. Nobody was around then. I think it was naptime. So, what should I do next? It's not even lunch time."

"Let me check. If anyone's around to check with. I don't feel like getting my head bitten off." Denny left the office and Elizabeth really had nothing to do. She'd only been trained to input files and without files, she was adrift.

"Might as well." She got out her pocket calendar and backtracked to dates when she knew fires had occurred and people had been hurt. She entered the date of the North County fire in the report number window. That came up, which meant the report had been misfiled. It was making her crazy that dates and report numbers had been entered wrong. Clearly, someone wanted to hide the reports of the fires, but why? There were probably 20 to 30 people involved in each fire, so it's not like other people didn't know about it. What piece of information was someone trying to hide? She began a list of the injured fire fighters, and the fires in which they'd been hurt. She'd have to check with Tig and see what they had in common. She didn't know any of them very well, except for Terry. She knew Brian Espinoza a little. They'd met at some department barbeque or another. She remembered his cute little wife. Newlyweds, she thought. Even in high heels she only came up to Brian's shoulder, and he wasn't all that big. They were still in the 'smitten' part of the relationship and couldn't hide it. Nauseatingly adorable. Elizabeth had liked her right away and had a feeling this marriage would last.

Okay, Brian on the list. How to find other fires? Hmmm. Hunt and peck, she guessed. As she attempted to get appropriate reports, she realized how clever someone was. It was extremely difficult to score a hit this way. She had to admire it on one level. It would be so hard to *prove* anyone was trying to hide something. She knew how difficult it was to input the form correctly, and once it was entered wrong, the data base did not lend itself to searches. You had to know where to look. Even if you input the date of the incident, unless you put it in the report number window, you *still* wouldn't come up with the info. Pretty genius. Then try to prove it. Her admiration trickled away as she thought of the fire fighters who'd been hurt.

At least no one had been killed. Was that just luck? Any of the accidents could have been fatal. Fires were so unpredictable and humans so fallible. Almost all the fire fighters worked second jobs. Look at Tig and Captain Macbeth. One day you work too much and then get a big fire, your defenses are down, just that much and poof. Someone's dead. If Miranda hadn't heard Tig calling, a couple breaths more of smoke and . . .

She stopped herself right there. Not helpful. Okay, back to the reports. It figured that if a report came up when she entered the date in the report number window, that was probably a suspect report. If no report came up, then perhaps there was no report number like that, or that it was correctly entered. Easy enough to check. She picked a date and

171

entered it. Nothing. She took that date and put it in the date window. Medical call. Okay. Not all dates were report numbers, so she got a few misses, but enough success to feel like she was onto something.

"What are you doing?" Denny was back and stood where she could clearly see the screen.

Think fast, Elizabeth. "Just practicing."

"Practicing what?" Denny set a file box on the desk.

"You know, getting familiar with how things are done around here." Great answer. Dork.

"What for? You know your job is temporary."

That was kind of mean. "I know. But I am so awful at this." Go for pitiful and humble. "I just want to do a better job. So much depends on this data being correct, you know? Besides, won't there always be a need for data entry?" *Not like I'll work here ten seconds more than I have to.*

"No, once we're caught up the reports will be filed by whoever's in charge of the call. Aren't you a conscientious one?" Denny did not look terribly pleased by Elizabeth's excuse.

"I guess it's just me, then. If I'm going to do something, I want to do it the best I can." The first honest thing she'd said in the last five minutes. Change the subject.

"Do you think I could go to lunch before I tackle these?" She didn't actually report to Denny, but wanted Denny to think she was respected. In fact, Elizabeth wasn't sure how she felt about Denny. On the one hand, she seemed nice and thoughtful and a

172

good employee. On the other, why was she never out at calls? If she was a recruit, why didn't she go out on training? She wore a uniform. Something else going on, maybe. *I'm seeing crime everywhere,* Elizabeth thought sourly.

"Sure." Denny had resettled at her own terminal and was hard at work, acting like the previous conversation was completely forgotten.

Elizabeth grabbed her purse and texted Tig on the fly. She desperately wanted OUT of there for lunch. She hoped Tig could join her if he was up to it. After a morning's grilling, he might want to go home.

He responded to meet at the cars in fifteen minutes. He was just finishing up in the classrooms.

She waited in her car, not wanting to see anyone else right now. She was not so lucky. Joey came out of the offices and edged around the parked cars. Elizabeth slid down. He looked back and forth, the classic guilty guy, went to a white Tercel, and slipped something under the windshield wiper. He left quickly. When he was out of sight, curiosity consumed her and she had to see what it was. A note. She opened it and read, 'I'll be waiting for you.'

"That could mean anything or nothing." She replaced the note and went back to her car to wait for Tig. She relaxed against the headrest. "God, what a morning." She did feel a small spurt of satisfaction about her investigations. Whatever they meant.

She forgot Joey when she saw Tig. He was always handsome, but now she watched for clues about his morning. Did he look pale? Stressed? In pain?

She opened her door and got out so he'd see her. A quick kiss.

"How are you doing?" she asked.

"Exhausted. This was every bit as fun as anticipated."

She knew he meant his interviews with the brass about the fire.

"Are they satisfied? I mean, are they done with you?"

"I think so. I reviewed all the prep we did. I obviously couldn't speak as to the overall training, but my part jived with Miranda's report. All the set up was by the book. We're always super careful with recruits since they have no experience and can't be depended upon to react well mid-call."

"Hungry?"

"Starved. Let's take both cars. There's no way I'm coming back here today."

"You look a little beat."

"I feel like I've been hit with two by fours for an hour."

"We can skip lunch if you just want to go home."

"Nope, I don't want to make anything, that's for sure."

"Italian Deli?"

"I'll follow you."

Elizabeth drove to the busy parking lot of the Dollar Store which also housed several restaurants and a large grocery store. They had to park away from their favorite deli, and Elizabeth again voiced concern for Tig.

"Are you okay to drive home after this? I could take you and we can get the car later."

"I think I just need some food and I'll be okay."

They both ordered salad combos from the counter girl, choosing different types of salads from the case so they could share. Tig loved the asparagus and Elizabeth was partial to the marinated mushrooms, but everything was so good it was hard to choose.

They got their own iced teas and sat at an outside table in a little arbor.

"I did some more research this morning," Elizabeth said. At his raised eyebrows she added, "only on computer and in the data base where I'm allowed to be." He nodded.

"It's really hard to search because it's not set up to search for certain types. I mean, I typed in 'injuries' and nothing came up. Then I entered dates of fires where I knew someone had been hurt. That worked, so I made a list. Will you check it and see if you can tell what they might have in common? For the life of me, I can't tell."

She handed him her list and he carefully scanned it. The counter girl brought their plates and he put the paper aside. Appreciative noises were all they exchanged for next few minutes.

Elizabeth rose with her glass. "More tea?"

Tig nodded, mouth full of asparagus. She refilled their teas at the dispenser and when she returned, Tig was perusing the list.

"I really can't see anything that links these guys. Some I don't know, but for the most part, they're different ages, ethnicities, stations, length of service. It's just really hard to see what might have gotten someone riled up. I don't even know what questions or whom to ask."

"Rats. I was hoping you'd know more. Okay, let's take you and Terry and Brian. And is there anyone else you know on the list? Just you guys. What do you have in common?"

He looked again. "I just don't know." He handed her the list. "All our wives are hot." He smiled.

"Oh, you think their wives are hot, do you?"

"No, I think MY wife's hot."

"Good recovery." She leaned in for a kiss.

"I'd like to pursue this discussion, perhaps later in the privacy of our own home. And after a nap," Tig added.

"We'll see how optimistic you are later, sailor." They stood and disposed of their trash.

At the cars Elizabeth hugged him tight. "Oh, sorry. Did I hurt you?"

"Only in a good way." He looked tired.

"You feel okay to drive home?"

"Yes. Going straight home to the cat-nurses. I'm glad I went back to work. At least the grilling is over for now and maybe tomorrow I can catch up on paperwork."

"Okay. I expect to be home around six. I'll make dinner. Don't do anything." A last kiss and she got in her car and drove to Division.

176

Back in the office, Denny said, "Cove called and you can get the files today. Go at end of shift and then just go home. I know you live out that way."

Elizabeth sort of lived out that way. Cove City was on the right side of a geographical Y, her home and Bay station on the left side, and Division way down at the bottom of the base. Denny was being thoughtful, so she thanked her.

"Oh, I'm supposed to call County and make a finger print appointment. I'd better do that. Maybe I can do it today and make one trip instead of having to go out again tomorrow."

"Mmmmm," was the response from Denny.

Elizabeth set up a print appointment for an hour later. She calculated thirty minutes to get to the County office. Then however long the prints took and maybe twenty minutes to Cove station.

Once again, she had nothing to do without new files. At this rate she'd be out of a job sooner than she thought. Maybe not a bad thing.

"Can I help you with anything?" she asked Denny.

"No, it's faster if I just do it."

Okay. She pulled out her list again. Tig was right. The fire fighters she didn't know, she didn't know what to ask. She couldn't say, *Hey Denny, tell me everything there is to know about Jim Downey.* That's not suspicious at all. She sighed. Maybe it was all coincidence. It couldn't be. Edward had seen someone run way from the house fire, and the animals at the North County fire had shown her a similar figure. Maybe she needed to go to the site of

177

the recent warehouse fire and interrogate the animals there. She smiled a little at that. Animals tended to stay in their hunting and homing grounds, but she didn't know if that was the case when an area was damaged or destroyed by fire. One way to find out. She had the warehouse fires files at home. Easy enough to visit the sites sometime. See if there were any 'witnesses' left.

Time to get to her print appointment. She gathered her purse and coat. "Bye, Denny. See you tomorrow."

She got another mmmm for her trouble. *I wonder if I'll figure her out.*

On the highway out of town the skies gradually grayed up as she neared the coast. She felt her spirits dampen with the atmosphere. The County lot had spacious parking so she got inside in plenty of time for her appointment. They were able to take her right away. She was surprised to find her prints would be taken by computer, inkless, and sent to records that way. *More computers!* The days of ink and cards seemed to be past. At least here.

It took several tries before the technician was satisfied. She apologized and said, "If I don't do it right, they kick it back to me, and then I have to call you out here again. It's a pain, but better to do it this way."

"That's okay. Thanks."

Elizabeth made good time to Cove City and again parked right in front of the door, remembering how helpful they had about carrying the box.

She stepped into the same hallway, and was

met by a burst of laughter. No naptime today.

She followed the noise to the common area and entered to hear a familiar voice say, "What a bitch! Women are like that." A profound silence as she was noticed in the doorway.

The speaker, a large man in street clothes but unmistakable as a fire fighter said gruffly, "You should learn to knock," as he turned to face her.

"Captain Macbeth!" Elizabeth squeaked out. His angry face melted and his voice was immediately the kindly one she remembered.

"Oh, Mrs. Murphy. I thought you were some civilian wanting a tour. You know." He was very jolly and his arm extended as if to go around her shoulders. She backed up a step.

"I'm actually here on Division business. Came to pick up a box of records. Captain Jensen, I mean Mike Anselmo was getting them ready for me."

She heard mutterings of 'Captain my ass' etc. and figured the opinion Denny had of Jensen was shared.

"What are you doing here?" she asked Macbeth. "I thought Jensen was swinging in here for a while?"

"Just visiting."

Elizabeth heard the unspoken 'little lady' addition and wanted to smack him. He was well over six feet and two-fifty, so she didn't. He was older, but looked quite solid.

"Visiting. That's great." She didn't know why she felt so uncomfortable. She had visited Tig in his station lots of times and had always been made welcome. This was strange but she couldn't say why.

"I used to swing in here for quite a while before I got my own station. I still like to check on things and make sure they're doing their jobs." Much hale and hearty laughter.

Elizabeth just wanted out. This was her second visit to Cove station and she did not like it either time. The energy of this station was not right. To be fair, if Jensen was not a good captain, the men would be unhappy and it would show. She would ask Tig what he knew about Cove station. And Jensen.

A handsome fire fighter came in with a file box. She reached for it but he said, "Let me get it for you. It's heavy."

Surprised, she said, "Thanks." She opened the outer door for him and unlocked her car. He set the box where she indicated. She saw now the name on his shirt was Anselmo.

"You're Mike?"

"Yes. Sorry about that in there." He seemed embarrassed for his station mates. "Uh, it's not personal. One of the guys caught his wife running around on him, and you know, we all sort of gotta show support. Even though he was running around on her first." He mumbled that last part.

"It's okay. I should have knocked, but it was so noisy no one would have heard me. It's no big deal."

"If you need anything else, just ask for me."

His eyes twinkled and he smiled, but it didn't feel like he was flirting with her. Dark hair slicked back caught the sun and she saw his appeal for the ladies. She liked him, too, but not in a man-woman way. Just a nice guy. On impulse she asked, "Do you know Tig Murphy?"

"Oh, sure. Good guy. We've done some training together since we're both senior men." His face showed query.

"He's my husband. I just wondered. Maybe you and your wife would like to have dinner some time?" Why did she say that? Now he'd think she was flirting with him!

"Thanks for the invite, but I'm not married. Haven't met the right one." He winked and she got the impression he was happy with lots of 'ones'.

"Oh, okay then." That was close. What was she thinking? Tig didn't need her to make friends for him. She got into her car and Mike returned to the station.

She couldn't put her finger on it, but his energy was strange too. It didn't really fit in Cove Station's odd atmosphere. She didn't find him personally appealing, not her physical type, and she was madly in love with her husband, but still. Something about Anselmo tugged at her. Oh, well. Let it go, it will come.

Twenty-Two

At home Elizabeth threw together a big Greek salad. As she was setting the table, Tig and two cats wandered out of the bedroom, all looking sleepy.

"How are you feeling?" she asked as she set glasses of water on the table.

"Much better. Needed that nap." Tig sat at his place and yawned.

Me, too. I needed that nap, Teddy echoed.

Tough day, you two? Elizabeth asked the cats.

Yeah, said Edward. He clawed his way up Tig's leg.

You have to stop doing that. Can't you jump yet?

I don't know. Let's see. Edward jumped off and then back on again. *I guess I can!*

Tig sat silent, used to these exchanges. Elizabeth knew she got a funny look when she was 'talking' to an animal and whatever Tig thought, he was usually respectful.

As they dug into the salad, Elizabeth told him of her visit to Cove station.

"Mike Anselmo was pretty nice. He said he knew you?"

"Yeah, he's a good guy. Actually, he was at my station before all this started and we got to talking. We may study for the captain's exam together. I know it'd mean swinging for a while until something opened, but you know, if you never try. . ." His eyes sought her approval.

"Of course, you have to try. At least that puts you on the list for a station, right?"

"I might not get one around here, that's the thing. It's an area-wide test, so if I pass, I prioritize my stations. I could get something in the North County, even as far as San Domingo." A town sixty miles away.

"Gotta do what you gotta do, right?" She smiled at him and took his hand. "What would make you happy? Staying close to here, or being a captain?"

"Both."

"I know, but 'prioritize.'"

"Captain means more money. More money maybe means a family, or a really good car." He laughed and she knew he was kidding about the car. They'd talked about a baby for some time but didn't feel they would be comfortable financially, even with his landscaping and her work with animals.

"I was thinking maybe I could contribute a little more," Elizabeth said. She definitely didn't want to work at the grocery store or sling fries, but there must be something she could do with animals. She'd have to research it. The zoo, maybe? For her, even cleaning up after animals was preferable than interacting with people.

Tig knew what she was thinking. They'd had this discussion before. "Don't worry about it now. If we need that, we'll do it when the time comes. For now, what about Cove station and Anselmo?"

"Nothing about him specifically, except he was the only nice person at Cove. Both times I've gone there it was business. I mean, I wasn't there to get a tour. Really frustrating. And if I was there for a tour, I'd sure be disappointed in what I saw."

"What?"

Elizabeth explained. "And what about Captain Jensen? Is he as bad as they made him sound?"

"I've heard rumors, but I've not had any bad experiences when I've worked under him. What did Anselmo say?"

"I didn't ask. I just wanted the files and to get out of there. He did apologize for Macbeth. What's going on there? I thought he was so nice when Terry got hurt?"

"He's divorced and pretty bitter about it. His wife was having an affair or something. Anyway, that was a while ago, a few years? I think he's willing to show solidarity for any guy getting the same treatment."

"That's what it sounded like."

They cleaned up together and retired to watch Law & Order dvds.

Tuesday was the most normal day since the training fire. They got up together, had coffee and dressed. Over breakfast, Elizabeth explained the idea she'd come up with yesterday.

184

"Since you work half day now, I thought I'd take a half day and maybe we could go see the warehouse fire sites?"

"What for?"

"Okay, well." Elizabeth took a deep breath. Tig supported her animal sense, but asking him to participate and buy in to build a crime was another thing.

"I have the files here. I wanted to compare the two sites and also see if any animals are still in the area who might have seen what happened." The last part came out in a rush.

She could see him struggle not to laugh or tell her she was ridiculous. She didn't read people, but that was not too hard.

"I know. I know how it sounds. But what can it hurt? I know it's not evidence, but maybe it will give us something to go on."

"What do you mean, go on?"

Now she was frustrated. "Oh, come on, Tig. Aren't you curious? Don't you want to know if this is deliberate? You could have been seriously hurt or even killed and it's not a joke."

"I know that. I just don't think it's a crime. Other than arson. I don't think someone's out to get us. Fire fighters, I mean."

"Seems like a lot of coincidences to me." Elizabeth folded her arms.

"Or maybe we're getting lax in our training. Maybe we need to review things, write some new procedures, not hunt for a plot when there isn't one."

"Okay. Say you're right. What can it hurt to

185

see the fire scenes?" Elizabeth pulled out the two files and showed him the photos. They looked eerily similar, although they were years and blocks apart. "It's only the warehouses I want to check. It's not like it will take all day."

"That one," he pointed to a photo, "is completely gone. They razed what was left and I don't know if they've built anything there yet."

"That's okay. I just want to see the area for myself and also check. . ." she trailed off.

"I know. Witnesses." He sighed. "If I don't go, you'll probably go alone and I don't want that. All right. After work today?" She smiled and nodded. "Let's carpool then. Do you know if you can work only half day?"

"Don't worry about that. I'm getting good at it now. I don't think that'll be a problem."

"Okay. Saddle up."

At Division Tig carried her box into the office for her. She was a little relieved that Denny wasn't there to see it. She didn't feel like ogling or ribald remarks this morning. Joey wasn't there either. Maybe he'd been reinstated to full recruit status. She'd have to ask Tig. If so, perhaps Joey was getting smarter about keeping his mouth shut. If he was the guilty one, that was a bad omen for the department. If she didn't stop him, who would? Even her husband thought it was nothing. If only the animals she 'talked to' were more reliable witnesses. Sure, a dark figure, probably male, sometimes wearing a dark ball cap, at least once with the logo FIRE on it. Joey seemed dumb enough to do that. Or

186

maybe he figured that cap would make it seem like he belonged there? To offset any questions. A firefighter at a fire. Even if he was there early, he could claim, what? He smelled it and rushed over? Weak.

She sighed and opened her computer. This second Cove box was much better organized and the files were older. What had Jensen been thinking? Just keep Division off him for a while? Why? Covering something? I guess Jensen warrants a closer look, too.

She input data for two hours and then took a break. Something about the reports bothered her, but she didn't know what. Coffee. That's what was needed.

She'd been so busy she hadn't noticed Denny come in. There she was, typing silently. Very unlike the Denny she'd met at first. No loud chatter, bluster, jokes.

"Morning, Denny. Coffee?"

"Sure." Denny looked up. Her eyes were puffy and red. Allergies? Crying?

Elizabeth brought her a cup. "Are you okay?"

"Yeah." Her hand shook as she took the mug. "No. I don't know."

"Want to talk about it? What's going on?"

"I'm not sure. This guy I've been seeing. I thought things were really good, and then a couple days ago, bang, he is too busy to see me. No real explanation, just busy." She sipped her coffee. "And I don't know what's going on around here. Everyone's so uptight. I got hauled into the office to

187

talk about the training fire too, and I wasn't even there."

"I'm sorry. About your guy. Isn't he in insurance? Doesn't he look into arsons? I mean, he could just be busy. He works for a big company, right? They could be sending him out a lot. Not just here, maybe, but farther afield?"

Denny looked a bit hopeful. "Yeah. Maybe. But why wouldn't he tell me that? What he said was more like a kiss off."

"I don't know. I don't know him, but if you don't have a reason to think otherwise, maybe give him the benefit of the doubt?"

Denny took another swig. "Yeah. That's right. Maybe it's a lot of work. I guess I have to wait and see. Thanks."

"Beats getting wound up over nothing until you know for sure."

"That and getting reamed by the brass yesterday just about did me in."

"What did they expect you to know?"

"They asked how the training was prepped from the office end, and I really had nothing to tell them. I didn't do anything, I didn't even print out forms or memos. I'm not sure what they were looking for, but they made me feel like a criminal."

"I'm sorry. Can I ask you a personal question?"

Denny looked wary. "Sure."

"I see you wear a uniform, but I've never seen you go out on calls or participate in training. I just wondered."

Elizabeth felt like an idiot, and an invasive one at that.

"It's not a big secret. I am a fire fighter but I'm out on medical. I had my appendix removed and I'm on light duty for a while. I normally work out of a tiny station so there wasn't enough desk duty to accommodate me. They put me here, which I don't mind at all, or didn't mind, because it put me close to my sweetie. Who may or may not be my sweetie any longer."

"Denny, I'm sorry. I didn't mean to pry."

"Yes, you did. But it's okay. You're working hard here and you have a right to know who you're working with. Especially with all the excitement lately."

"Speaking of that, what's up with Joey? I haven't seen him around."

"He did so well at the training fire that they've rescinded his probation and he's back in regular recruit class."

"Good for him. I hope it goes well."

"Me, too. The guy's been an idiot. Okay, these files won't input themselves."

"I should get back, too. Oh, by the way, I'm leaving at one today, just a half day for me. I've got some stuff to do."

"Gee, it wouldn't have anything to do with your hottie hubby on half days, too, would it?"

Elizabeth turned scarlet.

"I hope so. One of us should be getting some."

Well, Denny was more like her usual self.

189

That was a good thing, wasn't it?

Elizabeth was more than half way into her box when she thought of something. She didn't see nearly the injury rate in these older files that she had with the new files, or with recent cases entered by someone else. She checked her numbers. She'd entered 53 cases today. Not bad! She took a moment to be proud of herself. Of those 53, all dated over three years ago, only about ten percent had any sort of employee injury or medical incident. Scrapes, smoke inhalation, one broken arm. She then reviewed the recent cases. That was more tedious since she didn't have paper files on them, and didn't know how to search the data base for particular statistics. She pulled up cases one at a time, putting the date in both the correct and incorrect windows. She went chronologically, every calendar day.

She didn't get very far before it was clear the recent injury stats were much higher. It seemed to taper off the farther back she went. She put in every day for a month, six months ago.

Then a year ago. Definitely a pattern of increasing accidents more recently. The reports were from different stations, so she was not the only one putting in data. Someone else, perhaps a fire fighter, and of course Denny, and maybe other file clerks had begun the process. Not to mention her phantom data input person. Obviously, some of the incorrect reports were truly accidental. She knew how easy that was. Maybe that was how he or she got the idea.

Now she had a pattern. What to do about it? That she still didn't know. A time check showed

190

nearly one, so she shut down, made a quick bathroom stop and met Tig in the parking lot.

Maybe a fast lunch was in order before she went to interview critters in a warehouse district.

She sighed. Sometimes it was hard even for her to live with herself.

A quick stop at Tacos de Mexico and Tig drove to the first warehouse, the earlier fire where the building had been razed.

A shiny metal structure, Quonset-hut style, had risen from the ashes. Industrial park type landscaping edged the property.

That was a good sign for animals. More cover, more places for them to make homes and find food. This site was at the end of a cul de sac near a radio station and kiddie gym.

Tig parked on the street and they walked from there. First she circled the building. Nothing exciting or unusual. She listened and heard leaves rustling from the slight breeze. The trees were the sort of Aspen-y type so popular in shopping centers. She liked them but they were noisy and masked any minute noises little creatures would make. They continued to the radio station and kiddie gym buildings, listening and looking. Nothing.

"Okay," Elizabeth said. "This is where I have to do my thing. I'm going to sit on that rock and see if anyone's willing to talk to me. You can't just stand there and watch me. Do you want to wait in the car?"

"I don't want to leave you alone."

"I'm sure it's fine. Even though this business," she glanced at the sign, 'A & M Welding',

191

"isn't a hub of activity, the others are fairly busy. I'll be fine."

Tig hesitated. "Okay. But I'm moving the car."

She knew she had to concede to that. She smiled and kissed him. "Thanks."

He looked surprised at her quick surrender, and started back to the car.

She sat on the flat-topped granite boulder and spread her feet apart, a good connection with the ground. She had left her purse in the car, but made sure her cell phone in its belt holster was off, not just on vibrate. She didn't want distractions. The boulder was in mottled shade under one of the rattle-y trees and the warmth of the sun, intermittent with the breeze and shade were soothing. She easily settled into herself.

A quick grounding and she sent feelers out in concentric rings. She felt much life around her as she sent out pulses of energy. She heard several 'conversations' but couldn't determine where they originated.

She began to 'call' for assistance with her problem.

What's in it for me? asked a voice.

Her mind cast around for the source and discovered a deer mouse similar to the one Teddy and Edward had found.

Depends. What do you know?
I know a lot.

Elizabeth asked about the fire. Showed mind pictures.

192

The mouse became afraid, but not the way an animal who had that bad experience would become afraid. It was afraid of fire, as all animals were. Elizabeth wasn't sure how she knew this distinction, but she did. She probed the mouse a bit more and discovered it was too young to have been at the fire. She didn't know how long mice lived. Especially with all the predators.

She explained it was too young to help her with her problem and thanked it.

Do you know any older animals around here?

Don't care. With a flip of its tail, it was gone. She had to laugh. She opened her eyes and felt the earth, re-acquainting herself with here and now.

She walked back to the car and got one of the granola bars she kept for emergencies. "Be right back," she said to Tig. Back at the rock, she crumbled the bar and tossed it around.

"Enjoy," she said, and returned to the car.

She buckled up. "Nothing here. I guess this fire was too long ago for anything to still be around. Let's go to the next."

Tig drove to the site of the recent fire. A similar street that also ended in a cul de sac. Instead of the freeway, a creek bubbled behind the buildings. They proceeded as before, both doing a walk around. The building had been burned to a skeleton and the neighboring buildings appeared to be abandoned, or at least businesses with no foot traffic. No stylish landscaping either. Whatever felt like growing there was left to its own devices to battle it out with other

193

plants. Nothing green was between the building and the street, all of it having burned. The burn area continued to the creek bank, but the fire fighters had been able to protect the neighboring businesses from damage.

Near the structure, what was left still smelled faintly of fire.

Tig could wait in the car with Elizabeth in full view. He grabbed a soda crate from a nearby building and upended it for her to sit on.

Again, she grounded and explored. Because she had just done it, it was faster to connect this time. She got a lot of response to her energy search. The creek was abundant with life and since the fire was so recent, many of the creatures remembered it. She suspected most of the remaining energy was insect in origin, because she only got fragmented pictures, no continuity and no words of any kind. A scratching in her brain reminded her of the cockroach invasion and she abandoned that line of energy, searching for a higher life form.

A fluttering near her. She opened her eyes, but kept her energy open. When she contacted animals she almost always had her eyes closed, but some animals were very strong in their communication to humans. She could 'talk' to them much like she 'talked' to Teddy or Edward. Edward was not as able as Teddy, but he was learning.

A crow flapped at her feet. Glossy black and as big as a football, he stood on strong-looking legs. He eyed her sideways. He was not afraid and energy poured out of him, powerful and rascally.

Hi, she said.

I hear you. What do you want?

I need help.

I like shiny. This was not entirely a non-sequitur. She had worked with crows and ravens, and a few other species of birds before. They always wanted payment.

I have something shiny. Do you remember the fire?

See shiny.

Elizabeth pulled a jumbo paperclip from her pocket.

See shiny, she agreed, but didn't put it where he could take it.

Fire? A questioning energy. He was asking what she wanted to know about it, not questioning the fire itself. She read that he had been near the fire.

Show me the beginning of the fire. She got pictures of the building at night. No exterior lighting, which she thought was odd.

Light? She sent a picture of the building with lights on.

No light. He sent a picture of the buildings again, none of them had lights in the cul de sac. No moon, making it very dark. She only could see because he could. She doubted she could have seen anything with her puny human vision, had she been here.

What else? Humans? Show me how the fire went. She closed her eyes, better to concentrate on his pictures. He was a little distracting, like a kid strutting up and down in front of her, pausing to pick

195

up something or fluff his feathers.

His energy sent a fast series of pictures, more like a child's flip book than a movie. She saw from the bird's perspective as it moved around the buildings with all his distractions and caution. She could follow the story, because he was very smart.

Again, the rarity of olfactory sense. She smelled the fire as the crow had. She saw the wisp of smoke rise and smelled it. The crow's heartbeat increased and he flew to a tree farther from the building. His eyesight was excellent and she was able to track the fire's progress. The smell increased and became more acrid, but it seemed a very long time before she saw the first flame. The crow had been aware of other animals leaving the area. Rodents and insects and small birds fled from the building, but the crow's curiosity kept him near. He flew to another tree and from this perspective she saw the dark human figure in the shadows who grasped something in his hand. A large something. She wanted the crow to move closer so she could see what it was, but he didn't. She despaired of any helpful information. She was about to disconnect and thank him, when the building burst into full flame and the light allowed her to see the figure more clearly. Backlit she could not see his face, but she could clearly see what was in his hand. An electric saw. She knew what it was because Tig used one all the time. Not a chain saw or a circular saw, but a reciprocating saw used for cutting beams, walls, doors, lots of things. It wasn't proof, but the roof had fallen in on this fire, after men had been ordered in. If

Tig had not refused, the collapse could have killed him, and anyone sent in with him. Now she knew the building had been sabotaged. The cut beams had burned in the fire, leaving no evidence of tampering. Sure it was arson, but so were a lot of fires. This fire had been rigged to make the roof fall.

A moment after the fire flared up, the crow had enough and flew farther away. She never saw the person's face, and this time there was no logo she could read.

She was shaken and took her time coming out of her meditative state. She opened her eyes to see the crow still at her feet. He hopped and rustled his feathers.

Shiny?

Yes, shiny. She thanked him and gave him the paperclip. She felt a surge of joy from the crow as he picked up his treasure and flew away.

Back at the car she told Tig what had happened.

"You look a little pale," he said.

"I feel kind of woozy. That was scary. If you had followed orders, you probably would have died."

"I know."

"But now we know it's sabotage. My heart is racing."

"What that crow told you is not evidence."

She checked his face for the scorn she sometimes got, even from Tig. Not there.

"I know. You sound different."

"It's just that I've never really seen you work

before. I know you talk to the cats all the time, but most people talk to their pets. I just take it for granted that the cats talk back to you, even though they don't to me. It's not so strange. This was different. I sat here and watched that crow come right to you. I saw him stay with you for minutes. He looked right at your face, even when your eyes were closed. It was weird. I got such a sense of back and forth between you. I didn't see your mouth move, or his beak or whatever, but I could almost see the flow. I can't explain it." He took her hand. "I guess a little part of me thought, maybe you were exaggerating or well, not making it up, but I don't know."

Elizabeth nodded. "I know. It's odd to you. It's a little odd to me, too. I just trust it. It's not very practical as a skill, though, is it?"

Tig looked in awe of her. "I don't know anymore. It's pretty special. I'm sorry for the times I may have acted skeptical."

"It's really okay. I have a question for you. When you guys checked out the building, or the arson investigator did, was there any exterior lighting? The crow showed me the buildings in complete darkness and I wondered. Seems strange for these businesses, isolated the way they are."

"I don't remember any lights that night. The building was fully involved when we got here. We were just trying to save the other buildings and the brush from catching fire. If all these grasses had burned, wow."

Elizabeth saw the lack of landscaping as a sinister addition to the arsonist's choice of targets.

No lighting, or was that sabotaged too? She would check before they left. And lots of dry fuel. The area had had a wet winter, good for growing all the grasses. By summer, the fuel load was high and the fire could easily have gotten away from them. It wasn't far from houses and other industrial buildings. She leaned in and kissed Tig.

"What?"

"I just thought about all the lives and property you saved."

"Just doing my job, ma'am." He looked pleased.

"Before we go I want to check these other two buildings for outside light fixtures."

"Sure. Let's go." They locked the car and went to check.

"Looks like there were fixtures at one time, but not now," Elizabeth said, looking up above the main door way.

"Yup. It was removed and not gently. Looks like someone smashed it off with a sledge hammer. Maybe recently. Not a lot of rust or weather damage, looks like from here. Hard to tell." He squinted at the remains of the fixture.

"Let's check the other building." They crossed the burn area to the other structure and the same thing appeared to have occurred.

"Why would the owners let this go? Wouldn't insurance insist on a repair?" Elizabeth asked.

"Yeah, if the owners knew about it, maybe. Unless it was an insurance fire. They could try to make the lights seem like vandals and the same for the fire. I've seen them do it to security cameras, too. I didn't see any camera stuff, but maybe one of the fixtures was a light/camera combo."

"It seems our arsonist chose his properties carefully. Maybe he knew these buildings were abandoned or had absentee owners who wouldn't check them regularly," Elizabeth said.

"Did your crow show you anything about the damage to the lights?"

"No, everything was dark when he got there. But the old fire, that other warehouse? That had booming businesses on either side. Why would he choose that? From his perspective, this area is perfect for not getting caught, but that one seems high risk."

"That fire happened three years ago." They walked back to the car. "Maybe those businesses weren't there three years ago, or that structure cave-in really was an accident. I don't know."

"It should be easy to check on those businesses. I've been listening to that talk radio station for years. Dave Congalton is my favorite, so that's not new."

"I don't know." Tig unlocked her door. "You can check right? On the data base?"

"It's not going to show me the area businesses three years ago. I'll have to go downtown to do a records search. They're not on computer either." Elizabeth smiled. "I guess we're not the only ones still in the 19th century."

"What will that prove anyway?" Tig pulled

out onto the main road.

"I don't know. I can't imagine what those records will show, but maybe our fire bug really was active that far back? Or practicing? Even if he cut that roof too, there's no way to prove it now."

"We have a lot of suggestion, but no proof of anything," Tig said.

"He's really smart. I don't think you're going to catch him unless you're extremely lucky. Like he flips out and confesses."

"I know. We'll have to catch him at it, I guess." At least Tig sounded like he believed something beyond arson *was* going on.

"I hope we do before he kills someone. These accidents seem to get more dangerous and violent."

On that sobering thought they drove home in silence.

Twenty-Three

Wednesday dawned bright and sunny and Elizabeth couldn't believe how it lifted her mood.

She and Tig drove separately since she had to put in a full day. He told her he felt fine and would get a doctor's okay to return to work full time.

She told him she would take her lunch break downtown so she could check the business records for that fire three years ago. Tig was right, she didn't know what it would prove, but she wanted to know.

Division bustled with training activities. Drying hoses festooned towers and dark blue figures hustled back and forth on various tasks.

Denny seemed in good spirits and Elizabeth asked what the amping up of activity meant.

"Recruit class is finishing this week. Next week they get tested on everything. Whoever passes, gets booted to a station. The rest can try again. Except Joey. This is his last shot. He must be nervous."

"I would be. If this was his dream, he would be a wreck. He seems like he's tried to pull it together this week. Do you think he'll make it?"

"Might at that."

"If he doesn't pull anymore crap, you mean?"

"He has some issues with authority, but so far

he's been okay. He's perfect when it comes to procedure. He practically has an aneurism if he can't coil the hoses perfectly."

"Maybe he should be a captain," Elizabeth said, half joking.

"That's all we need. Another anal captain."

"What do you mean?"

"Never mind. I gotta learn to keep my mouth shut, too."

"If it's Jensen, I've heard."

"Yeah. Well, it's going around."

Elizabeth didn't know if she meant news about Jensen, or more than one captain was being criticized. Denny's closed face deterred further questioning.

"Sorry for being a pest, but I saw Joey leave a note on your car. I hope he wasn't harassing you."

Denny looked blank. "I didn't find a note. I wonder what that was about?"

"I sort of read it. I didn't want him bothering you."

"What did it say?"

"'I'll be waiting for you.'"

"I never saw it. Where did he leave it?"

"Under your wiper. You drive a white Tercel, right?"

"Yeah. I wonder what it means. I didn't get the note, so maybe he changed his mind. He's in enough trouble as it is. I know he's not too crazy about me, but maybe he decided to grow up and fall in line. He's been doing much better."

"Maybe." Elizabeth wasn't convinced.

203

Maybe Denny did get the note and was lying. Ridiculous, why would she do that? Too much thinking.

She opened the data base and began the tedious chore of data entry. She kept glancing at the clock. As in all tedious things, time stopped and it seemed forever before she could go to lunch downtown and do her records search. At 11:30 she'd had enough.

"Going to lunch." She grabbed her purse and heard mmmmmm from Denny.

In her car she tuned in the talk radio station. Downtown was close, but too far to walk, check records and then return to Division in an hour. She passed the new court building in her search for parking. She had just scored a metered space when she heard on the radio, "Don't forget to join us in our two year anniversary celebration starting next week. We've been in our new digs for two years now. Next week we'll have lots of special guests and promotions, one of which is lunch with one of our hosts. You pick the host, we pick the restaurant. Six lucky people will join us next week for lunch, so stay tuned for more."

"Well that answers that question." So they weren't there three years ago. "What an idiot," she scolded herself. Again, if she'd thought it through for five minutes she could have had her answers sooner and with less hassle. It consoled her some that Tig didn't think of it either. She opened the phone book she kept in the car and looked up "Gymber-Jam", the kiddie gym near the radio station and the site of the older warehouse fire.

"Gymber-Jam, where your kids rule!" was the perky greeting.

"Uh, yes, I just have a quick question. How long has your business been at the current location?"

"I'm not sure!" Just as perky. "Did you want a brochure for your child?"

"No, I just want to know how long you've been there."

"Okay, hold on!" A clunk as the phone was abandoned.

Elizabeth heard a babble of children's voices, and deeper voices she hoped were adult supervisors. All in all, it sounded chaotic. Not having or working with kids, Elizabeth was unsure if this was a good thing or a cause for alarm. As she pondered this, someone picked up the phone.

"Hello, this is Marjorie. How can I help you?" Not perky, businesslike. Elizabeth was relieved.

"I wanted to know how long your business has been at its current location."

"Why?"

Why. An excellent question. Elizabeth hadn't planned an answer for that and she wasn't a good liar. So, the truth. Sort of.

"I am looking into the fire in the building next to yours and wondered if you sustained any damage."

"Oh. Well then. No we didn't because we weren't here then. The owners put up this building after the fire. I guess six months or so? They built at the same time the burned building was replaced. They got a good deal since the construction crew was already working on the new building."

"Thank you very much." Elizabeth hung up quickly before Marjorie asked for credentials.

She crossed the street to Thai River and ordered take out. While she waited she drank hot ginger tea. Usually she didn't like sweetened tea, but this was ambrosia, sweetened with ginger syrup. One of her treats.

She went over everything in her mind. She came to several conclusions. The arsonist was clever and vindictive. His plans were not specific, in that he didn't seem to care who got hurt, as long as someone did. She had no proof. Not one piece of solid information to take to anyone in command. And who would that be anyway? She suspected everyone, because nothing pointed to one person. It saddened her to think it was a fire fighter, but after the training fire, she just didn't see how it could be anyone else. His attempts were getting riskier. The warehouse fire had missed since no one was willing to go in. Tig had refused an order, but had not been written up for it. She knew because he would have told her. Insubordination was big on the list of offenses. Maybe this was because it was clear if he had followed orders, someone would have been hurt. That would have looked really bad for the captain in charge of the scene. Who was that captain, anyway? Tig hadn't said. At big fires, several stations responded, sometimes even the CDF, County fire did, too. It could have been anyone of them. The first

206

on scene is usually in command of the whole thing. Mental note to ask. Her food was ready so she finished her tea and paid.

Back at her desk, she ate slowly, relishing the flavors. She ate three bites more than she had room for, as was her habit, unfortunately. She consoled herself that veggies and rice digest quickly. She felt her phone vibrate on her waistband. Text from Tig. 'Doc apt 2day 3pm'

She hoped he'd be cleared to return to full duty. A medical clearance meant he was really okay, and, he was champing to get back to work. When the recruit class finished, he'd go back to work at his station. That was what he really loved.

Denny had been gone when Elizabeth returned, probably having her own lunch. Now she breezed in with a file box. "More goodies!" She was definitely feeling better. "I think we're seeing the light at the end of the tunnel."

"Great." Elizabeth had mixed feelings. She wouldn't miss mind and butt-numbing data entry, but she had enjoyed being close to Tig's world, and the paycheck that would result. She didn't know if she should tell Denny about the mis-entered data. Denny was there on temporary status, so maybe she should see a captain? A chief? Someone in Human Resources like Connie? She just didn't know. For now, she wouldn't tell anybody about the data, since that was her one thin, but concrete thread to something being wrong. However wispy that thread was.

"What a freaking mess!" Denny stared at the

contents of the box.

"What's wrong?"

"Just look at this! It looks like someone spilled a pot of coffee on the whole thing. How are we supposed to read these? And they stink!"

Elizabeth took a folder and opened it. It was badly stained and a little furry with mold. She wafted it under her nose. It didn't smell too bad, but the box reeked.

They removed the file folders, banging them against the metal trash can to rid them of dirt and clumps of mold. They stacked them in two piles, sharing the load.

"Uh, oh, that's the problem," Denny said. She lifted a folder and pointed.

"Ugh. Poor thing." A mouse had gotten into the box and given birth, then been unable to get out. The family had died together, hence the stench.

"Gross." Denny dashed out the office door and returned with the spray air freshener from the bathroom.

"Good idea." They removed the rest of the files and dumped the mouse remains in the trash. Denny sprayed individual files, fanning them back and forth with gusto. Elizabeth propped open the office door hoping the smell would dissipate. Denny took box and trash can out to the dumpster.

Elizabeth noticed the last few files had been used to make a nest for the mice. The mouse had chewed through several layers of files in the area that currently most interested her. Namely the date, case number and person in charge of each scene. The bottoms of the reports still had signatures, stained, spotted and fairly illegible. She hoped they could be deciphered.

Denny returned and liberally sprayed the office trash can. "Well, that was fun."

Elizabeth smiled. "And now, back to our regular programming. By the way, where was that box from? What station?"

"File storage here." At Elizabeth's expression she laughed. "Oh, yes. We still have many, many boxes to do."

"I thought we were doing really well. I thought those boxes we put in Classroom 4 were it? Do I want to see the storage room?"

"Nope, you certainly don't. Don't worry, though. You and I are not responsible for all of it. We are just catching up some of the backlog, and we'll be done after next week's recruit tests. I go back to my station and the budget runs out for you. At least that's what I heard. Unless you want to apply for regular Clerk I?"

Did she? "I'd have to think about it." Coming here every day, completing mindless tasks? The job so far had had two forms. Frustratingly impossible the first week, and incredibly boring the second. Gee, tempting.

They agreed to input the smelly files first and get them out of the office. This was slow going since the documents were so damaged and difficult to read. Their hopes of completing them in an afternoon were dashed. The box had been pretty full. *That mouse was certainly determined to make her nest there*, Elizabeth thought. She'd climbed her way to the bottom of the box and then chewed through the files to make a little den. The newborn mice couldn't get out the same way, and for whatever reason, the mother had stayed. Maybe she died after giving birth? Who knew. At any rate, the mouse had made the job more difficult. Squinting for hours through spills and crud gave her a headache. By five they were both more than ready to quit.

"Should we leave these files here? They're pretty stinky," Elizabeth asked.

"We could put them in the captain's office for safe keeping." Denny winked.

"You're terrible! I didn't even think of security, but you're probably right." Denny hooted laughter. "I don't mean in the captain's office, but someplace safe. I didn't lock up the files I was working on before. I feel terrible."

Denny said, "I just put them in the desk. No worries. It's safe here. The office is locked after hours."

Yeah, but who has the key? Probably a lot of people. Nothing had happened to the files that she knew of. But one or more could have been removed. Since they weren't in the computer system yet, no one would be the wiser. So many people came and went from Division on a daily basis, and this week it had been a zoo with all the brass, admin, recruits, regular employees. Well, there wasn't a thing she could do about it. She felt stupid for not thinking about it before. Especially since she was the one with all the crime theories.

"What are you thinking about?" Denny asked with the interest that showed how much Elizabeth must have revealed on her face.

"Just what a dork I am. I mean, one of the reasons we're doing this is to make the information more secure, right? And there I am, leaving files out in the open for anyone to see."

"Don't worry. Jeez, it's not military intelligence, it's fires and old people with heart attacks."

"I guess so." Denny's reaction reduced Elizabeth's suspicion. Unless she was a really good actress. Elizabeth hadn't seriously considered Denny though, anyway. But good to know. Elizabeth was sure someone was going to a lot of trouble to hide his crimes.

They shut down and walked out together. Today they had parked close to each other and Elizabeth saw a parking permit in the lower corner of Denny's windshield. She hadn't noticed it when Joey had left his note.

"That's your car?" she asked Denny.

"Yup. Cute isn't she? Great mileage."

"Are you starting college again?"

"What?"

"Your parking sticker, is it new? I didn't see it before."

"No, that's old. I just haven't taken it off. I'm lazy. I took Spanish there, thought it'd help me on the job. It does, but man it was rough."

"Oh." Elizabeth thought hard. She pictured Joey lifting the wiper and placing the note. She should have seen the sticker. That meant it wasn't Denny's car. That was why Denny didn't get the note. "Does anybody else here have a white Tercel?"

"Sure, Miranda does. We sort of bonded her first day, both having the same car and being women. I know how hard it is. I gave her some support, you know. Said come talk to me if she needed anything. She never took me up on it though. Everything I've heard through the grapevine says she's doing great. Gonna graduate near the top of the class. The guys bitch that she's not as strong, but you know, she's fearless. The first to volunteer for anything. I think she's gonna be fine."

Elizabeth agreed. She remembered her conversation with Miranda at the hospital. Miranda was the reason her husband was alive.

Pulling in the drive at home, Teddy and his shadow, Edward, sat by the front door. Tig's car was there, so he was home. She was eager to hear how his appointment went.

She put her purse on the table. "Smells good in here," she called. Tig came out of the kitchen and kissed her.

"My famous chili."

"You are feeling better."

"Got cleared to go back to work. I'm to help with testing for the recruit class next week. I think that's why I got okayed. My shoulder is still a little sore, and they don't want me climbing ladders yet, but bossing kids around I can certainly do. After next week, I'll be returned to full duty."

"Yay!" Elizabeth hugged him. "I'm starved.

That smell is killing me."

"Okay, we're ready then." He dished up bowls of fragrant chili ladled over brown rice. He pulled garlic bread from the oven and carried it to the table.

"This is so good," Elizabeth mumbled around her first spoonful.

"Now you sound like me." Tig looked pleased.

Elizabeth caught him up on her day and then asked, "Who was in charge of the scene when you were ordered into the warehouse and refused to go?"

"Chief West."

A chief. She hadn't really considered a chief in her list of suspects. She supposed it was possible since there were usually chiefs at a scene. She didn't know enough about procedure.

Tig continued, "But it wasn't West who ordered us in. West is a good guy, level headed, calm. He suggests you do things, like you have all the time in the world to run hose out. He's great to work with the new kids. They get so excited and flustered, and he just brings down their level of anxiety. But, no it wasn't him. It was Macbeth."

"Macbeth? Why would he do that? I thought he was one of the good guys?"

"He is. Well, was. I don't know. I used to really get along with him, but he's different now. More tightly wound. This is his second career and he's getting up there in years. I think he wanted to make chief, but it looks like captain might be as far as he's going to go."

"Why can't he make chief?"

"There's only so many openings for chief and Macbeth is close to sixty. Someone's gotta die before he'll get it," Tig joked.

"If chiefs were targeted by the sabotage, then we'd have a suspect. I guess it's not Macbeth. I just don't see a motive for him. Unless getting divorced is a motive."

"Probably not. Half the guys have motive then. They're either divorced or on second marriages."

"I know. At Cove station he was so. . . angry, I guess is the word. I'd never heard him like that before."

"He hides it pretty well, I think. He doesn't want 'regular' people to know. We all know, but he tries to stay professional. His wife was having an affair with a fire fighter from another station. It took him a while to figure it out, but then he went ballistic. Sad because he really loved his wife. Now I hear him dissing wives and women in general. He champions the guys whose wives he deems aren't good enough."

"That's what I heard. Anselmo told me Macbeth was supporting a guy whose wife was fooling around on him. Then added that the guy had done it first."

"I don't think that matters when you're so hurt. I guess Macbeth figures she deserved it. I don't know. I'm glad we're not like that."

"Me, too." They held hands across the table, the cats as usual, Teddy flopped on the floor, and

Edward in Tig's lap.

Twenty-Four

Thursday was bright and sunny again and the shared drive to Division was positively gorgeous. Tig drove and Elizabeth gloried in the view they passed on their way to town. Rows of bright flowers filled the fields: yellow, orange, white and her favorite, hot pink.

The Division lot was full again, so they parked down by the picnic table.

"Maybe lunch here later?" Elizabeth asked.

"I didn't bring anything. I'll check my schedule and maybe I can pick up something."

"Text me, because maybe I can. I think my really important job can wait." She kissed him hard. "That's a promise for later."

"Wow. I like later. Let's have later now."

Elizabeth laughed. She loved his sense of humor. "No, later is for later. That's why it's called later."

She left Tig at the classrooms and continued through the building to the main office.

Denny entered just as Elizabeth was removing her jacket and stowing her purse in the desk.

"It doesn't smell bad in here. I thought for sure it would."

Elizabeth nodded and pulled the files from her desk. "Yes, not so bad today. I've got about a dozen reports to decipher. How about you?"

"Me, too. Yesterday it took forever to get through one 'cause I couldn't read half the information," Denny said.

"I'm going to start with the hardest to read. Maybe that will help psychologically if it gets easier as I go."

"Good idea."

The morning progressed in near silence. Their only conversation was when one or the other asked for an opinion or clarification.

Elizabeth stretched. "My neck is so tense from reading this mess. At least I'm done with the mouse files. How close are you?"

"Couple more. I think I got more mouse-nest files than you did. These are pretty chewed up."

"Give me one, I'll help finish."

"Nah, I'm stubborn. You can go get another box as penance." Denny tossed her a key ring. "Go onto the apparatus floor. At the far side, back, there's a locked door, unmarked. That's storage. The biggest key. Go downstairs and all the way down the aisle to the last cage. Red key opens that cage."

Cage? That sounded ominous.

"Does it matter what box I pull?"

"Not really. I grabbed a box from the back, and maybe that's why it was a mouse house. Just grab any box. Make sure you lock the cage though. They get really pissy if a cage is left open. They store everything down there."

Elizabeth found the door and went down stairs dimly lit by low energy lighting. It was chilly down there. At the bottom, endless rows of cages stretched before her. It seemed the storage area took up the entire acreage of Division, underground.

More yellowish light showed her the 'cages'. Individual chain link boxes, each with its own padlock. She passed equipment, both new and ancient. Boxes of medical supplies, tires, uniforms, all manner of things, both useful and, for all intents and purposes, junk. Some items looked like they belonged in a museum. Of course, document storage was all the way back. The red key, difficult to see in the yellow light, fit and turned the lock. She was relieved to see Denny had exaggerated the number of boxes remaining. She grabbed the closest one, probably a recent addition, and set it outside the cage so she could relock it, bearing in mind Denny's admonition.

The box got heavier as she reached the top of the stairs. Elizabeth made a mental note to request help the next time she needed a box. She hoped not soon. Like after recruit class graduation, when she no longer worked here. *Probably won't be that lucky; I'm getting so good at this.*

Back in the office she and Denny perused the box contents and divided the work. No mouse house, so it went much faster. This box was not stuffed to the edges as the other had been. The reports dated from ten years earlier, when the local population had been considerably smaller.

Nothing grabbed her attention until

cacophony from the yard penetrated her concentration.

"Come on, let's go watch." Denny streaked out the door. Curious, Elizabeth followed.

In the yard behind the classrooms, an aerial truck sat, ladder fully extended. Recruits gathered near the truck, receiving instructions. One by one, they were expected to climb the ladder.

Elizabeth was not surprised to see Miranda head for the ladder first. From her vantage point, she saw Miranda's face, pale and tense, but with a look of determination. She climbed slowly but steadily upward. The ladder moved with her weight and Elizabeth held her breath. When Miranda reached the top the watchers cheered, sounding like they had been holding their breaths, too. Elizabeth was pleased to see support for the one female recruit. It couldn't have been easy to make that climb. Elizabeth couldn't have done it, she knew. She heard Tig's voice in her head, "Unless there was a kitten at the top." She smiled and clapped as Miranda came down safely.

Next, several men successfully reached the top. She noticed the crowd moving a bit and watched carefully. She saw Joey move toward the ladder each time someone came down, but it seemed he couldn't quite make it to the line. His hesitation might be an issue. Only a few men to go, and so far, no one had failed the ladder test.

Miranda moved next to Joey and spoke to him. He nodded and moved purposefully, cutting off another recruit. His ascent was markedly slower than

219

anyone else's the higher he went. Elizabeth felt for him. She had trouble in buildings over ten stories high, and that was just in the building, not hanging off a ladder.

Instructors, including Tig, called directions or support up to Joey. Someone in the crowd started chanting "Joey, Joey" and clapping and the others quickly picked it up. After several agonizing minutes of start-stop, Joey reached the apex. The group roared. The ladder bobbed as he slowly began his downward trip. When he reached the ground he was clapped on the back and congratulated. He wore a big smile. It was the first time Elizabeth had not seen an underlying look of calculation or defiance on his face. Maybe he would make it this time.

Denny cheered, one of the loudest, and Elizabeth saw Joey's look of appreciation at her support.

Elizabeth returned to the building. Now was a good time to get lunch for her and Tig. She texted him to let him know she would pick up the food.

She called an order to a small Italian restaurant that relied almost exclusively on take-out.

She input a few more files before she picked up the food.

Tig met her at the picnic table. The open lot was now empty and quiet. The aerial truck had been moved and the recruits were elsewhere, celebrating their success.

They helped themselves on paper plates and dug in.

"So good," they mumbled at the same time,

then laughed.

"Pretty exciting morning, huh?" Elizabeth asked. "How did it go from the instructors' point of view?"

"Everyone passed. Most of them will never be on an aerial truck, but it's part of the training."

"How's Joey doing this time? He hasn't been in the office and I took that as a good sign."

"He's made marked improvement. He might just make it."

"If he's not charged with arson, sabotage and attempted murder."

"There is that. I don't think he's the guy."

Elizabeth sipped her tea. "I wouldn't have agreed with you a few days ago, but either he's a complete sociopath and an excellent actor, or he was just afraid of not passing class again."

Tig nodded. "Now that he's wrapped his head around the chain of command, he really has some plusses. Time will tell."

"How are you feeling? Gonna make it through the rest of the day?"

"I feel great. Shoulder is tender, but if I don't jerk it around, it's fine."

"What's next this afternoon?"

"Reviewing for next week's tests, today and tomorrow. Should be no problem. Next week will be easy, proctoring written tests and monitoring the physical testing. Piece of cake."

"Good. I'm glad next week will be my last. This is getting old."

"I know, but it's been nice having you

nearby." They shared a smile. "Later," he said with his lascivious look.

Elizabeth laughed. "Later."

They cleared their trash and went their separate ways. Elizabeth entered the office with a feeling of dread. She was truly sick of this job. It seemed it had no end, and she did not like never-ending work. She preferred projects that gave a sense of accomplishment. Denny was absent, probably at lunch, so she had no excuse not to get right to it.

She finished her section of files and thought about starting on Denny's. She decided against it. Best to get a fresh box.

She grabbed the keys from the desk drawer and headed down to file storage. Still cold and poorly lit, at least she now knew where she was going. She opened the cage and decided to check the boxes instead of just grabbing one. Maybe she could organize, so the process was more efficient. She pulled out her cell phone to use as a flashlight and promptly lost her grip on it. It skittered under the wall into the next cage, which, she presumed, she did not have a key for.

"Shit," she said. She heard a chuckle and her heart dropped. Macbeth blocked the doorway of the cage, padlock and keys in hand.

"Hello there," he said.

"Oh, God, you scared me."

"I bet I did. What are you doing here? Poking your nose in where it doesn't belong?"

He looked enormous in the half light. "No, I

came to get more files to input. Denny and I have caught up with the other stations' files. Now we're on to Division's backlog." Why was she telling him this? He didn't really care.

"That's not all you've been doing."

"What do you mean?" She picked up a box like it was a natural thing to take it out of the cage. He didn't move so she had to put it down.

"A little bird told me you've been checking file entries for the last few years. Why would you do that?"

What little bird? She hadn't told anyone but Tig. Not even Denny. "I was just doing my job. I had a hard time learning the program. I made a lot of mistakes."

"Mistakes, huh? So why'd you keep going? Why'd you keep digging? What do you care about old reports?"

"Old reports that were hidden. It just seemed odd, that's all. Guys were getting hurt but the reports were buried. Why?"

Elizabeth backed farther away and risked a glance toward her cell in the next cage. She might be able to reach it under the bottom pipe. Her arms were slender enough. As if he'd let her try. He blocked the only exit, holding the keys and lock.

"How would you know and why do *you* care?" she added.

"First, you can't get your phone. Second, nothing happens in this department I don't know about. I put keystroke loggers in the terminals and I can see who is doing what on a computer at any time.

Someone has to take care of things around here."

"You still haven't answered my question. Why hide reports?"

"I don't answer to you. Who says they were hidden? You said yourself how hard it is to enter data correctly. What makes you think there's some plot here?"

"*You* said nothing happens here you don't know about."

"You're pretty emotional. Women shouldn't be here, and that's the truth. They go all hormonal and do weird shit. Here's your lock. You shouldn't leave it outside the cage. Someone could lock you in. It's not smart."

"Why did you follow me down here? Just to intimidate me? It's not like we're alone. People know I'm down here; what did you hope to accomplish?" No one knew she was down here. His appraising look said he knew that, too.

"Yeah, all about you. I came down here for supplies, saw the cage door open and came to check it out. Everything has to be locked all the time."

"Well get your supplies then. Stop blocking my way." Elizabeth picked up her box and he backed out of the cage.

"Let me take that for you."

"Now you want to help? Forget it. You can lock the cage if you're all up on security. Give me my keys back."

He was so tall and wide. This close she saw his beard stubble and smelled his sweat. He clearly did not like taking orders from a woman, but he removed the key from the lock and set the ring on her box. She turned and walked away on shaky legs with as much dignity as she could.

At the top of the stairs she realized she'd left her phone in the next cage. "Shit!" she repeated. No way was she going down there alone again. Maybe she'd get Denny to go with her. And take something to scrape it out with.

Back in the office Denny was typing in her own files. She looked up when Elizabeth came in with the box.

"Whoa, what happened to you?"

Elizabeth hoped she didn't look as upset as she felt. "Just getting a box from storage. Macbeth startled me. Gave me some line about not wanting women to work here. Kind of creepy."

"Yeah. He's a jerk. I warned Miranda about him. He can't do anything openly or HR would be all over his ass, but he sure pushes the limits. The Old Boy network in full force."

Elizabeth didn't tell her what he said about computer stuff. She didn't want to explain to Denny what she'd been looking for and why.

"Yes. I just need more caffeine. That'll do the trick." She didn't really feel like coffee now, she rarely drank it after her morning cup, but it was a distraction.

"You're in luck. Just made a fresh pot. Let's see what you got."

Elizabeth poured a cup while Denny sorted the new files.

Denny pulled a handful and tossed them to her own

work station. "I can't believe how well we're doing. Making great progress. We might get more done than I thought before we're both out of here."

"We're just too fabulous. Despite that vaginal handicap, we're managing. Although I do feel a little hysterical right now. Maybe I'll faint?"

They laughed and Elizabeth felt some of the tension go. Macbeth was a jerk, no doubt, and if the rumors were true about his wife fooling around on him, that could explain his attitude. Maybe it was no wonder his wife wanted out. Who knew? None of her business.

She got right to work and didn't stop until the coffee hit her and she needed a bathroom break.

By five she and Denny were dragging. The task was consummately boring, also taxing.

"One more day," Denny sang. "Tomorrow's Friday, tomorrow's Friday."

"I'll be glad for the weekend myself." Elizabeth quickly called Tig using the office phone to let him know she was done. She walked through the main building to the classroom wing on her way to the car. The classrooms were quiet now, the recruits gone for the day. Tig crossed the parking area toward her.

On the way home, she filled him in on her encounter with Macbeth. He looked angry enough to punch something. She was glad he was driving.

"Nobody treats my wife like that. That is his last chance."

"What are you going to do?"

"File a complaint. I don't know how many he

already has, but I don't care. His attitude is way out of control."

"It seems like he's the guy, doesn't it? What should we do? We still don't have any proof."

"Maybe I can talk to someone about it when I file the complaint. Someone who can look into it."

"Good idea. That's a relief. I wasn't sure what would happen down there. I didn't think he was dumb enough to actually attack me at Division, but you never know. When people snap they don't always make logical decisions."

Tig made a U turn.

"Where are you going?"

"I think we deserve a treat. Let's go to the Boar's Head Pub and then get some dinner. I haven't had a beer in ages and you love their hard pear cider."

"That's a great idea." They swung back into downtown and parked along the creek, several blocks from the pub, as close as they could get this time of day. They walked hand in hand and took a booth in a dark corner. It was cozy and romantic. They placed their orders when the barman came around.

"You know what is odd, now that I look back?" Elizabeth asked.

"What?"

"When Macbeth asked me why I was researching mis-entered files, he seemed curious, not mad. Like, why would anybody care? It seemed strange at the time, but I was so nervous I didn't process it until we were driving here."

"Maybe he wanted a chance to cover his tracks. Maybe he figured if you could find it, so could someone else."

"I guess. But it's all going to come out tomorrow. Friday should be really interesting."

They were enjoying their evening out so much they opted for burgers at the pub instead of changing locales. Tig had another beer. Elizabeth switched to water and agreed to drive.

By the time they came out, the sun had set. The evening was cool but not uncomfortable. As they neared their car, footsteps rushed up behind them. They split apart to let the jogger by. Elizabeth barely had time to register the man was not a jogger.

She heard Tig gasp, "Jensen!" before she was shoved to the ground. Tig was clubbed with something and fell over the embankment into the shallow creek.

The creek had high banks at this point and darkened buildings on either side. The open grounds of the Mission spread beyond the buildings but they were deserted this time of night. She took all this in in seconds.

Jensen had turned on her. "I should have done this a long time ago," he mumbled as he came at her. She had regained her feet and backed away on the sidewalk. They were blocks from the main drag and no one would hear her yell. She had a millisecond to think about Tig at the bottom of the bank. She prayed he was not dead or drowning.

Jensen's stubby hair plugs looked sinister and monster-like in the moonlight. He still wore a uniform. How could he get away with this in such identifying clothing? His attack could easily have been witnessed, what was he thinking?

"Captain Jensen? What's going on?" Her only hope was delay.

"I've been going about this all wrong." His eyes burned with empty intensity.

"What?"

"You bitches. It's all your fault. We get all wound up because of you and you do what? Mock us. Screw around on us. Make us a laughingstock at work. Then, you *invade* our work. The only place sacred to us. Now *you're* there, too. No escape, no escape." He had stopped to respond to her. She tried again.

"But what did you do wrong?"

"I, I, made a mistake. I went after the men. The guys. It's not their fault. It's YOU." He took another step. "Shoulda been you all along."

She took a chance. "Your wife had an affair, too?"

He made a growling noise.

"You went after fire fighters because she had an affair with another fire fighter?" She guessed this, based on what she'd overheard at Cove station. How common infidelity was! She was scared but she felt a wisp of compassion, too. Use that.

"I'm really sorry, Captain." She used his rank hoping some vestige of honor still resided in that messed up brain.

"You should be." He swung and she saw he used a golf club, sheared off at about two feet. Easy to conceal. Great. She pulled back and felt the whiff of passing air on her face.

"I didn't do anything!" She stumbled back again, and felt the bridge rail over the creek at her hips. No more retreat that way. Could she jump? It was about twelve feet down. Not too far, but the water was maybe a foot deep. Shallow enough to break a leg and then she would be a sitting duck. She saw a shadow behind Jensen. She tried not to react as Tig climbed up the bank. If she angled a bit, Jensen would not see Tig until it was too late. Keep him distracted.

"One thing, though, Captain. Why did you go after the happily married guys? They didn't do anything wrong."

Jensen stopped. Sadness passed over him, then was gone. "It was only a matter of time. I was saving them from my troubles."

"Saving them? Are you crazy?" He did not like the 'C' word. She was too mad to stop. "You put good men like Brian Espinoza, Terry Peterson, my husband and others, in danger to *save* them? Not every woman is like your wife. Or Macbeth's wife. We love our husbands. How dare you presume to judge what we do or don't do? It's none of your business!" She was shouting now, partly because she was so mad, also to cover the sound of Tig's approach. Jensen was taken aback by her tirade, but still looked mad and crazy. He opened his mouth and then folded onto the side walk. Tig stood over him with a river rock in his hand.

Elizabeth's cell still lay in the storage cage so

she gently took Tig's out of his pocket. Fortunately that hadn't gone in the creek. She dialed 911. She held tissues to Tig's bleeding head as they sat on the bridge, watching Jensen's still form, and waiting for help to arrive.

Twenty-Five

The darkened creek area filled with light and bustle as both police and fire responded. Elizabeth had called the police but someone, probably at a scanner, had notified the fire department. They took care of their own.

Tig was loaded into an ambulance and Jensen was cuffed and put into a squad car. Elizabeth would follow the ambulance on the short ride to the hospital. She was getting too familiar with that place lately.

Everyone ended up at the hospital. Jensen had to be evaluated before they'd book him. Ironically, Tig and Jensen sat practically side by side in the curtained cubicles of Emergency. Elizabeth was checked too, her scrapes and bruises deemed minor. The staff was more concerned with shock, but she passed that test. All she wanted was to sit next to Tig and hold his hand.

At last she was allowed in after they ran tests for Tig's head injury.

He was awake and alert. She kissed him. He smiled and her heart melted.

Dr. Georgiou entered with a chart. "Okay. Brain's good. No swelling, concussion, anything. Tough head." He smiled at Tig.

"So I've been told," Tig said.

"I think you can go home unless you have any concerns or questions?"

"No. Got a mother of a headache, though."

"Normal. I've got a prescription for pain. Should only need it for a couple days. If it continues, see your doctor."

"Thank you Doctor," Elizabeth said. "When can we leave?"

"Usual discharge paperwork, but also the police want to chat before you go. I'll let them know you're ready."

A moment after the doctor left the cubicle, two large, khaki-clad officers entered, entirely filling the space. Elizabeth rolled her bedside chair away as far as she could but it was still a tight fit.

The officers asked Tig for his story. She watched him. He seemed all right. She probably wouldn't sleep for days in case his head injury was worse than expected.

"Mrs. Murphy?"

From the tone, she thought they'd asked more than once.

"I'm sorry. What?"

"Can you please tell us what happened to you?"

"Aren't we supposed to be separated or something?"

"It's fine, ma'am. Just filling in the details for the report. You'll each get a chance to sign a witness statement and add anything you might have forgotten. You've both been through a lot so you can do that tomorrow."

I guess I do watch a lot of Law & Order. She felt herself starting to drag. The adrenalin had long since drained and she thought she could sleep for a week. *So much for not sleeping,* she thought. She told them her side as best she could. So tired.

"What will happen to Jensen?" she asked.

"Once he's cleared medical, he'll be booked into jail. From what you say, it's a pretty clear case of assault. Maybe attempted murder. We'll see."

"Of course it's attempted murder! He's been doing that for years!"

The officers exchanged a glance. The blond one said, "You want to elaborate on that?"

"You know I mentioned he said he made a mistake when he went after the guys? That he should have gone after the women from the beginning?"

"No, you didn't mention that he said anything. Only that he hit your husband and then came after you."

"Well, he did. I'm so tired I'm not sure I can make it sound sensible, but I'll try."

The demeanor of the officers had definitely become more official. "Maybe we should continue this at the station."

"Please let me take my husband home. I'll come in first thing tomorrow and explain the whole thing. It's rather complicated, and I am feeling a bit bruised." Why on earth had she opened this can of worms, now? She did feel exhausted but more than that, she needed to get Tig and herself into the sanctuary of their home.

"Give us the highlights then, and we'll decide."

She did her best to encapsulate the last two weeks into coherent speech. "I have documentation to back it up, but since I didn't know who it pointed to, it wasn't really proof of anything on its own. Is what he said to me a confession?"

"No, but it give us something to start with. He'll probably deny he said anything, unless he's a complete idiot."

"No, he's smart, but he's snapped I think. I think he tried all those years to hurt someone so he'd stop hurting, but it didn't work and he got worse. From what he said, it's only recently he decided that the women were all at fault. He's lumped all women into one conniving category and holds all of us responsible for his situation. I wouldn't have a woman interrogate him, that's for sure. He hates that women are in the fire department, too, so I doubt he'd respond well."

"Anything else for now?" She shook her head. "Okay, tomorrow, 9 AM, down at the station for a formal statement."

"Does Tig have to come that early? Can he rest at home?"

"He can come later, but you better be there. You don't want me to come looking for you."

"I'll be on time. Should I bring the documentation I mentioned?"

"Only what you already have. We need to get warrants for any files at the department."

"All right."

235

From the way they looked at her, it seemed she had crossed the border from victim to suspect. Not a good feeling. They went out and the tiny cubicle seemed vast.

Tig squeezed her hand. "It'll be okay. Let's go home."

Elizabeth hunted down a nurse who got them discharge paperwork and a wheelchair for Tig. A bit of déjà vu as she ran to get the car.

At home they did little more than fall into bed. Elizabeth was surprised to see it was only eleven in the evening. It felt much later.

After a thorough sniffing and final approval by the cats, the whole family fell into sleep. Elizabeth checked on Tig several times during the night. She woke him as directed and felt terrible for doing it. He was pretty good about it. He responded properly, so she let him finish the rest of the night in peace.

She wanted to let him sleep in the next morning, but knew she would worry if she didn't check him before she left for the police station. The cats snored through the whole thing and she felt immensely relieved at Tig's responses. She drove into town relatively satisfied. Her own bruises and scratches didn't bother her at all.

At the police station she began with the day she was hired. She was glad she had written down her progress through the files. It allowed her to explain her train of thought and omit the animal communication. She felt like a criminal. All she needed was for them to think they had a psych patient on their hands.

The officers thawed considerably as she told her tale. They had obtained their warrant but did not want her to accompany them to Division, for which she was grateful. She didn't want everyone to see her tromping through all the computer files with police officers in tow. Tig would have enough trouble when he returned to active status without everyone knowing she was the reason for the whole investigation. Up to now, no one thought any targeted crimes had taken place except arson. Jensen hadn't wanted anyone to notice. *I don't know how long he thought he could get away with it if someone died.*

She didn't mention Macbeth and his keystroke logger or anything else he did. The police would discover that soon enough.

By the time they let her go, it was afternoon. The warrant had been served and documents and computers seized. The officers who'd questioned her were not the detectives who would continue the case, particularly the cyber stuff. They had experts for that.

"Bring your husband in for his statement, Mrs. Murphy. Today."

"Yes, of course." She didn't know why, but they made her nervous. Even though she hadn't done anything wrong. Her experience was with fire fighters, not law enforcement. She hadn't even gotten a speeding ticket since she was 17.

She stopped at the store on her way back and got sandwich makings. She texted Tig and hoped he was awake to receive it.

Teddy and Edward waited on the porch. Some semblance of normalcy. Tig was up and dressed, watering plants out in the back. An excellent sign. She kissed him hello.

"How's the head?"

"Hard as ever. Had a headache when I woke up. The second time." He smiled at her, "A good dose of caffeine fixed that up right away."

"I'll make sandwiches, okay? Then drive you in for your statement."

"Sounds good."

They ate quickly, their usual relaxed conversation limited to necessary comments, each lost in his own thoughts.

At the police station, Elizabeth had to stay in the waiting room, while Tig was buzzed through.

She fussed and fidgeted, regretting not bringing a book. She cleaned out her purse again, re-checked her calendar, made notes of things she needed to do, like re-schedule that dentist appointment. She was making herself crazy but didn't know how to stop.

Finally Tig appeared looking a little worn.

"Can we go?" she asked.

"Absolutely. I'm hungry again."

Elizabeth hugged him. That was the best sign of his health.

"Want to barbeque? I've got burgers."

"Great."

At home, Elizabeth got condiments ready while Tig cooked. He was on his cell the whole time.

When he hung up he caught her up.

"Talked to Terry. He's back at work you know, and the whole county is in an uproar. The morning paper had a story. I didn't read it yet."

"Me neither."

"Jensen was behind the whole thing. He never got his own station and I guess that contributed to his deterioration. His wife started fooling around with another fire fighter, a permanent captain no less, and he really started to go. He was a swing captain, so he went to a lot of fires in different parts of the county. He was very mobile. He started sabotaging, revenge on the fire fighters, whether they were guilty of anything or not. So much happens at a scene, it's chaos. Every commander writes up his own report, but Jenson could easily modify computer reports to reflect his version. Who's gonna cross-check later? Jensen was able to write anything he wanted nearly unchecked. Then a couple years ago, maybe three? Macbeth got his own station, at a station where Jensen had swung into a lot and thought he was a shoo-in. Plus, Macbeth came to the department late in life and Jensen had been here since he was 21. That pushed him beyond his already unstable personality. He started targeting the guys, pretty much anyone, and then he went for happily married guys. Go figure."

"You'd think he'd have gone after the ladies' man types, wouldn't you?"

"I know, but he didn't."

"Last night he told me he was saving you guys."

"Saving us?"

"From your wives. He said he knew it was just a matter of time before your wives turned on you and started having affairs and ruining your lives."

"That's a funny way to save someone. Trying to kill him." Tig pulled the burgers from the grill.

"Just luck he never did kill anyone. Maybe he was trying to get them to leave the department and get away from the irresistible temptation for their wives—more fire fighters?" Elizabeth set the table and they sat side by side.

"Maybe. According to Terry, Jensen shifted gears again and decided it was really the women at fault, not the hapless and defenseless fire fighters. Apparently we are helpless against feminine wiles."

"I hope not."

"Well, I am against your wile." Tig smiled.

"Good, because I only have the one wile."

"And it's for me."

"It certainly is." She kissed him. She shuddered.

"What?" Tig finished his burger.

"Not you. I just remembered I was the first wife he decided to come after. And if you hadn't been there, I think I would be dead. He was crazy."

Tig pulled her to him. "Hey. Hey, it's okay now. We're both fine. Everyone's fine. They got him. And they wouldn't have if it hadn't been for you."

We've been waiting. A really long time, Teddy said.

Elizabeth looked down. The cats sat with

240

their tails curled around their feet.

I'm sorry. Waiting for what?

A piece of whatever that is. Cats love that.

Hamburger. Okay, here you go. Elizabeth hadn't finished her burger and broke off a bit for each.

Teddy inhaled it immediately.

Edward sniffed it. *That's all? Isn't there something else?*

I thought cats loved that? Elizabeth asked.

No, they don't, Edward said.

"Guess what," Tig said.

"What?"

"It's later!" He pulled her to the bedroom.

"So it is," Elizabeth said and closed the door on two indignant cats.

Victoria Heckman is also the author of the *K.O.'d in Hawaii* mystery series and the *Coconut Man Mysteries of Hawaii* books. She divides her time between California and Hawaii. Visit her website at: www.victoriaheckman.com

www.ingramcontent.com/pod-product-compliance
Lightning Source LLC
Chambersburg PA
CBHW020800250626
47155CB00003B/1156